MAID
OF THE ABBEY

by

ELSIE J. OXENHAM

COLLINS
LONDON AND GLASGOW

Copyright
First printed in this edition, 1949

DEDICATED
TO MY SISTER
MAIDA
ON THE DAY WE BOUGHT
OUR LITTLE HOUSE

PRINTED AND MADE IN GREAT BRITAIN BY
WM. COLLINS SONS AND CO. LTD.
LONDON AND GLASGOW

CONTENTS

6 CONTENTS

CHAPTER I

A RAPTUROUS PROSPECT

" IT's a rapturous prospect!" Lindy sighed, as she lay in bed on the first morning of the holidays —holidays which meant a new beginning for her, for she was just seventeen and she was not going back to school. " But I wish Nan had told me more about it. Things seemed such a rush last night."

She looked at her sleeping sister in the other bed. Anne was eight years older than herself, and she had been working for some time. The question was—what work was Lindy going to do? Some job would be necessary, and she knew what she wanted to do—what she would give all the world to do. But Nan was sure it was impossible.

" We'll see about that!" Lindy vowed. " If you want a thing badly enough—and I do!—you ought to be able to get it!"

She had come home late the night before. There had been supper and some hurried unpacking. Anne had spoken of a strange invitation for these holidays, but had put off full explanations till the morning and had insisted on bed, saying she was too tired to tell more.

" She looked tired, too," Lindy said to herself, gazing at Anne's brown head, so unlike her own fair curls. " She's frightfully white. She hasn't got over that bout of 'flu, in spite of this fortnight she's had on the moors. And she coughed a lot. I don't like it; she's not well. I expect it was a shock when her shop went flop, and she hates having no job; but she'd find a better job if she was more fit to look for it. Perhaps this new idea will put her right. I wonder when she'll tell me? *I know!*"

She slipped out of bed and, in dressing-gown and slippers, made for the tiny kitchen. The flat was very small, just two rooms and the bathroom and kitchenette, but it had been big enough while Belinda was at school and Anne was out all day at her cake-shop.

" But if neither of us finds a job, we shall be bumping into one another all the time," Lindy groaned, as she put a kettle on the gas-ring. " It's horribly pokey, after school!"

A vision of long dormitories, airy classrooms, wide corridors, breezy sands and playing-fields, and the naughty juniors to whom she had been a stern but much-loved prefect, swept before her eyes. She squared her shoulders and prepared a tray for early tea.

" School was all right while I was a kid, but now I'm grown up. I've left; I'm going to find a job, and some day I'll make everybody talk about me!"

She did not look grown up, with short fair curls round her face and a frank boyish grin. Beaming with pride, she carried the tray to the bedroom.

" Nan! Wake up and talk to me!"

Anne turned over and lay staring up at her. " Lindy! I'd forgotten you were here! Oh, how nice of you to make the tea! But what a surprise, Belinda!"

Lindy laughed. " I'm not usually the little angel in the house, am I? But I must make you talk somehow, and I thought tea might do the trick."

" Oh, I see! Now I understand," Anne mocked, as she sat up. " Clever of you, Lin!"

" Put this round you." Lindy arranged a red dressing-gown about her sister's shoulders. " You were coughing last night. You're not very fit yet."

" No, my cough won't quite go. I enjoyed the time on the moors, but it was very cold. Perhaps I was hardly ready for it."

" Tell me about everything!" Lindy curled up on the bed and took her cup. " You were too seedy to write much. It was that typist girl downstairs who wangled the holiday for you, wasn't it?"

" She'd been to this big house on the edge of the moors, The Grange. It's run as a hostel, for giving country holidays to working girls, by some awfully decent people who live in the south and don't need it themselves. It belongs to Lady Marchwood; it was her home as a girl, and she had the idea of inviting people from Sheffield and Manchester to have holidays in the house. It's looked after by Miss Rowney, and when she heard my name she said it was the same as hers, only her Ann has no ' e ' on the end and she's called Nancy. She was very kind, but she was busy getting the house ready for painters and I didn't see a great deal of her. Nell Jones, the typist, had stayed there, and when she found how seedy I was after 'flu, she wrote to Miss Rowney and asked if I could go. I was sorry to have a holiday without you, but I had to go when I was asked. She only just managed to fit me in before the workmen arrived."

" The moors would be a bit bleak in March," Lindy observed.

" Yes, it was very cold and I was unlucky; I didn't have much sunshine, and I was craving for sun. Miss Rowney saw that; she's very understanding."

" And she proposed this other rapturous plan for both of us?" Lindy pleaded for the part of the story which concerned herself. " You told her about me?"

" When she invited me she asked if I had any sister or friend who could come with me, so I told her you wouldn't be home till the end of March. The night before I left she had a talk with me. She said she was sorry she couldn't ask me to stay on, and have you too, because she felt I needed more holiday, in better weather than I'd had, but with painters coming in it just couldn't be done. And then she told me of another hostel of the same sort, in a village in Oxfordshire, belonging to friends of Lady Marchwood, and said she had written asking if they could take both of us for two or three weeks. The spring flowers will be out in the south and there's much more likely to be sun and mild weather. It sounds perfectly heavenly!" Anne shivered and sighed.

" But what perfectly heavenly people!" Lindy exclaimed. " Do they all spend their time giving people holidays?"

" It's a lovely thing to do. I'd do it if I had the money. I don't like taking holidays from people I've never heard of," Anne owned, " but this sounds so entirely delightful that I couldn't say anything but—a thousand thanks."

" I should think not! Except perhaps a thousand million thanks! Oh, glorious!" Lindy sighed in ecstasy. " Two—perhaps three—weeks in the country — primroses — violets — hawthorn—cowslips! It's too good to be true! And to-night there's my birthday treat! Oh, what a mass of thrills!"

" We ought not to spend money on concert tickets," Anne said. " Your birthday present ought to be something useful, like a new summer coat. But I knew nothing would do for you but the music."

" Coat!" Lindy cried scornfully. " I'd go about in rags rather than miss *Gerontius*!"

" You wouldn't like it if you had to do it," Anne observed. " It's all right; I've bought the tickets. But next year's treat you must earn and pay for yourself."

" Nan, darling, isn't there *any* hope?" Lindy asked wistfully. " My training, Nan! Can't we afford it somehow? I can't go into an office!"

" Not the training you want, Lin. It just can't be done. Only the very best would satisfy you," Anne said firmly. " It seemed impossible before, but it's still more out of the question now. We must wait till I've found another job and till you've earned something to help."

" But it will be too late! Oh, Nan dearest, find some way to manage it! I can't waste my life!

Every one says I'll do well! I'll pay you back!"

Anne shook her head. " No good, Lindy. We simply haven't got the money. Don't keep on teasing. Think about to-night instead!"

" To-night will only make me feel worse," Lindy groaned.

" It's a pity I took the tickets, then."

" Oh, Nan, I didn't mean it! I'm dying for to-night!"

" Well, don't upset the tray. Better take it away and let me dress. We've a lot to do, if we're to be ready to start on Saturday."

" The day after to-morrow?" Lindy gave a shout. " I didn't know it was to be so soon."

" The sooner the better," Anne retorted. " We both have to find work, but we can't do it till after this holiday."

" What's the place called?"

" Whiteways. It's a village, beyond Princes Risborough, between High Wycombe and Oxford, with beechwoods all round."

" Whiteways is a pretty name. I wonder if the roads are all white? I say, Nan, if you'll swear not to think about having no job—not once, till we're home again—I'll not say a word about my career and my training. We'll have a holiday and forget all our worries. Will you?"

" I'll try," Anne promised. " It won't help either our holiday or our future jobs for us to keep on bothering about them."

" It will help the holiday if we don't," Lindy said vigorously, as she carried away the tray.

" Saturday! I can hardly believe it! And to-night there's the Free Trade Hall! I must hear that girl sing again; she was marvellous at Christmas, in *The Messiah*."

For two years now her choice of birthday and Christmas treats had not been a theatre but a concert, and she had heard—from cheap gallery seats—the best singers and the best music. Always she tuned in the portable wireless to hear London, and in this way she had listened during the Christmas holidays to *The Messiah* in the Albert Hall and had been fascinated by the singing of the contralto, a young half-Italian girl who was taking the solos for the first time. When Lindy had heard from Anne that this same girl was coming to Manchester to take the part of The Angel in *The Dream of Gerontius,* on the very day after her return from school, there had been no doubt of her choice of her birthday treat. Nothing else would satisfy her; she must see Madalena di Ravarati, not merely hear her as a voice; and she must hear the rich deep contralto sing the beautiful music of The Angel.

Lindy went about all day in a happy dream, and as she helped Anne to look over clothes, and mend, and pack for the trip to the country, her thoughts were not on her work but in the Free Trade Hall, where no doubt preparation for the evening performance was in progress. Dr. Robertson was the conductor; he would certainly insist on a rehearsal. And no doubt Miss di Ravarati would want one too, to get used to the hall. Did you say " Miss," with a name like that? Or should it be Signorina?

"Some day," Lindy said firmly, "*I* shall sing in the Free Trade Hall! And the Albert Hall and Queen's Hall in London too. Somehow I'll get that training; I *will*! I *must*! Some day Dr. Robertson will conduct the orchestra for *me*! But I shan't be The Angel, and that's a fact."

Her voice was a strong and clear soprano. She had sung all her life and had always been called on to take the solos in school productions. Her music mistress and singing master had promised her a great future, if she worked hard and had good training. She would pay for first-class teaching, they had assured her.

But where was the training to come from? Anne was firm and unyielding. They had only their earnings to live on; Lindy's school had been expensive and had swallowed up most of their small capital. It was necessary that she should begin to earn at the earliest possible moment. Singing could wait; she was only just seventeen.

Lindy felt it could not wait. Every week spent in any other pursuit would seem wasted. She had argued fiercely during the Christmas holidays, urging that when she left school at Easter she should, somehow, be trained as a singer.

Anne had been determined. Lindy, bitterly disappointed, had been difficult; had at times been almost impossible to control. Anne had dreaded her next return from school, with the problem immensely deepened by the fact that she was not to go back and must now decide what she was going to do. Her own difficulties had been increased

by the failure of the cake-shop for which she had
worked and in which she had had a small share.
It had closed its doors; her share had vanished and
she had no job. She had very little capital behind
her, after seeing Lindy to the end of her schooldays.
No doubt another job would turn up; she was well
trained in every sort of cooking and there were
always posts to be had. But at the moment her
future was uncertain, and she was not feeling able
to face its difficulties. All through her time of 'flu
and convalescence, as she struggled to keep on
working while still unfit to be up and about, and
all through the fortnight's holiday in the rather
bleak moorland hostel, which would have been so
lovely in the summer, she had been burdened by
the approaching return of Lindy, and the know-
ledge that the argument, the pleading, the tears,
would begin again.

" Miss Rowney thought me odd; I could see it
by the way she looked at me," she had said to herself in the train, on the way back to Manchester.
" But she didn't know what a load there was on my
mind. I'd have liked to talk it over with her, but I
couldn't discuss Lindy with a stranger, however
kind she was."

So, dreading the struggle with the little sister,
she had welcomed more than ever the unexpected
invitation to the hostel at Whiteways. It meant not
only a longer holiday, with in all probability sunshine and spring flowers and the warmth for which
she craved, but also a postponement of their difficult decisions. For Lindy, in new and delightful
surroundings, would be thrilled by the novelty

and beauty into which she would be plunged, and would be happy and easy to handle. So Anne hoped, and was intensely grateful to the unknown friends who had made the second holiday possible.

CHAPTER II

A THRILL FOR LINDY

ONCE more Lindy lay thinking in the early morning, but to-day her mood was quieter, for she had not slept much. The beautiful music still rang through her mind, and before her eyes in the darkness had been the picture of the singer who had been The Angel: a slight, small girl, white-clad, very dark, with great black eyes which looked far beyond the Free Trade Hall as she sang.

" She was lovely. I must hear her again, often," Lindy thought. " I shall listen-in whenever she broadcasts; it will be quite different now that I've seen her. I read in the paper that she was singing in *Elijah* soon; I wonder if they'll have wireless at this Whiteways hostel? Sure to have, I suppose; but there may be other people who won't want *Elijah*. It would be awful to know she was singing and not to hear her! There's the postman. I wonder if Nan's awake?"

She glanced at her sister, who had not moved. Lindy snuggled down and decided not to move either.

" I was up first yesterday. I'm sure Nan slept better than I did; she liked the concert, but she wasn't as thrilled as I was. I wonder what the post-man brought? It might be for me; one of the girls might have written. . . . I suppose I'd better see," and she rolled out reluctantly. " Nan isn't going to move, evidently!"

She came racing up from the front door and hurled herself on her sleeping sister. " Nan! Wake up! A letter, and the postmark's Princes Risborough! Perhaps it's to say we can't go to the village, after all!"

It took a moment to rouse Anne, who had been sound asleep and was indignant at this rough awakening. But when she understood she tore open the letter in anxiety as keen as Lindy's.

" No—yes—it is that—but it's all right," she said incoherently.

" Tell me, or give me the letter to read!" Lindy raged.

" I *say*!" Anne was staring at the signature. " This will thrill you, Belinda Bellanne! But the letter—yes. They've had a case of measles in the hostel. They can't ask us to go there, but they don't want to put us off; the country's looking so beautiful, and they know we'll have made our plans for leaving to-morrow. Considerate people! It would have been awful to have to give it up now."

" Sort of dashing the cup from our lips," Lindy agreed. " Jolly nice of them to see that! Are we to go somewhere else? Let me see, Nan!"

Anne lay back and gazed at her, still keeping the letter from her. " They suggest we should come and stay in their house—Abinger Hall. There's almost nobody at home—just some children and the secretary; and they've heaps of room. They're sure we'll be friends, because of the way Miss Rowney wrote about me; they'll let us feel as free to please ourselves in what we do as if we were in the hostel. Lindy! An invitation to a big country house! We simply haven't clothes for it!''

" Oh, rot!'' Lindy shouted. " They won't dress for dinner if it's only kids and a secretary. Our summer frocks will do, and as it's in the country jumpers and short skirts will be all right. Who are ' they '? Whose house is it? Whose secretary and kiddies?''

Anne looked at the letter again. " Lady Quellyn's; but she's in New York. This says: ' Miss Devine, Lady Quellyn's secretary, will look after you.' It was someone called Devine who wrote the first letter.''

Lindy's eyes widened. " Sir Ivor Quellyn's house? Oh, I *wish* he was at home! How I'd love to see him!''

" This says: ' Lady Quellyn's house,' '' Anne objected. " I suppose he's in New York too. What is he doing there? You know all about the musical world!''

" Conducting an orchestra; I read it in the paper. He went last summer,'' Lindy said promptly. " He was at home in the autumn for some concerts, but he went away again after Christmas. Lady Quellyn's house—and we shan't see either her or him! That's rotten luck!''

" Apparently we shall see her children and her secretary,'' Anne observed.

" But wouldn't she take her children with her? Won't it be somebody else?"

" We'll find out when we get there. It's marvellous to be asked to the house! I'm a bit scared," Anne admitted.

" But if there are almost none of the family at home!" Lindy argued. " Kiddies don't count; they must be only tinies. Lady Quellyn's quite young still. You couldn't be scared of a secretary! It's just terribly kind of them to ask us."

" You haven't asked who wrote this letter."

" Isn't it from—oh, but it speaks about the secretary. Then who——? Nan, tell me! Why are you hiding the letter?" Lindy plunged forward to seize the paper.

" Don't do that! You'll tear it, and then you'll be sorry. You'll want to keep it in a glass case. I'll show you, silly," and Anne handed her the letter.

Lindy gave a gasp of blank amazement. " It couldn't be! ' Madalena di Ravarati '—Nan! It couldn't possibly be!"

" I don't see why not." Anne lay and gazed at her. " And anyway, it looks as if it *is*. Didn't you tell me Miss di Ravarati had been brought out as a singer by Sir Ivor Quellyn and that she often sang Lady Quellyn's songs? Perhaps she's a friend and lives with them."

Lindy's eyes filled with awed expectation. " Do you think we'll see her? Speak to her? Oh—Nan! What a thrill! Does she say she'll be there?"

" She says: ' I may have to be away for a day

or two, but Miss Devine will look after you.' That
sounds as if she lived there."

" And as if she expected to be there when we
arrived!" Lindy shouted.   " We *shall* see her!
We'll be able to tell her what a lovely Angel she
was! But she's here in Manchester, Nan!"

" She was here last night. But if that was only
for the concert she'll go home to-day."

" And be there to welcome us. Oh, it's super
marvellous!" Lindy sighed in ecstasy. " There
isn't anybody in the whole world I'd rather see!
I might have been scared of Sir Ivor and Lady
Quellyn, but The Angel didn't look a scrap fright-
ening, did she?"

" I thought she looked frightened," Anne said,
laughing. " The Free Trade Hall's quite large
and she was rather small. She looked nervous until
she began to sing. She seemed to me very natural
and without any sign of swank. Her letter sounds
friendly; we needn't be shy. It will be wonderful
to meet her."

" You'll give me the letter?" Lindy pleaded.
" I shall keep it for ever."

Anne handed her the letter with a mocking smile.
" Here's the precious autograph. I shall tell her
you're carrying it next your heart."

CHAPTER III

MAIDLIN DI RAVARATI sat on the steps which led from the terrace to the drive before the Hall, her eyes on the beech avenue. Which of her expected guests would arrive first?

" I hope it will be the girls," she said to herself. " If I'd given them tea and sent them off to unpack I could take the others into the Abbey. But if the car from town comes first I shall have to wait for these Bellannes. It's an odd name, and ' Anne Bellanne,' who seems to be the grown-up one, is odder still. What was it Nancy said about her?"

She had read Ann Rowney's letter carefully several times, but she glanced through it again.

" My mind's still rather full of Manchester," she thought. " Odd that the girls come from there! I might have met them and brought them back with me; but as I was with the Robertsons, of course that wouldn't have been possible. How kind Mrs. Robertson was! She took care of me like a mother in that hotel. Now what does Nancy say about Anne Bellanne?"

She read the letter thoughtfully.

" ' Dear Maid,—Could you be good to a nice girl who's just had 'flu? I've had her here for two weeks, but it's been bitterly cold—we had snow while she was here—and she really wasn't much the better for it.' "

"I remember all that part." Maidlin turned a page. "It was something Nancy said at the end. This was it! 'I'm sure she has some trouble on her mind, but I couldn't get her to open out to me. I tried, but I really hadn't much time; I was busy preparing for the workmen, and I feel I failed with this girl. I can usually coax girls to tell me their troubles, and sometimes I think I help them a little.' I'm sure she does!" Maidlin interrupted herself. "Nancy would help anybody. But this girl evidently didn't respond. I wonder why she thinks I can do it, when she couldn't. It's all in this last sentence, of course. 'Maid, I sometimes feel you've absorbed something from the Abbey, its history or atmosphere, that makes you able to help people. You seem to have a big share of its spirit, and now that the others have all married and gone away, I believe you try to do your turn of helping people who come there in need. Do you do it consciously, or is it just chance? Anyway, do help Anne Bell-anne, if you can! Get out of her what the trouble is; even if you can't advise her, it will do her good to talk. She looked as if she was carrying a burden. Pretend you're the Father Abbot of the Abbey, and coax her to confess to you! She'll go away happier, as well as better in health. Perhaps she needs comforting. The little sister may be the difficulty. Mary Devine could help, in that case; she had trouble enough with her young sister, I believe. I know you'll be a good angel to the Bellanne girls! I shall listen when you sing The Angel in the Free Trade Hall.' Some day I shall have to tell Nancy what Rosamund and I feel about the Abbey."

Maidlin folded the letter, looking thoughtful.
" There's nothing unconscious about it! I try fearfully hard to carry on as the others used to do.
That's partly why I asked these girls to come here,
when the measles happened; I don't see what else
I could have done, but Nancy's letter made it seem
really necessary. If this Anne is in trouble—well,
isn't that why people used to come to the Abbey?
For help and refuge and comfort; I wonder if I'll
be able to help!"

She sat up and listened. " That's a car in the
avenue. Now am I going to have a muddle of
people all at once? Oh, it's Frost! Good! That's
one problem solved."

She ran up the steps and called into the house.
" Tea for three, Edith, please!" Then she stood
by the stone balustrade watching the car, which
she had sent to the station to meet the strangers.

Their first sight of her, as Frost drew up, was of
a slight figure in rich blue against the old grey stone
of the Hall; dark eyes gazing at them quietly, blue-
black hair coiled on her neck. Then, with a start,
she ran down the shallow steps to greet them.

" Do forgive me! I've been wondering so much
what you were like! I went off into a dream; it's
a bad habit I have. I'm so glad to see you! Did
you have a nice journey? You must be Miss Bellanne, but I haven't heard any name for you—
you're just the little sister!" and the dark eyes
smiled at Lindy. " Don't you have a name?"

" I'm Linda—or Lindy—or Lin." Lindy's eyes
were devouring her in rapture.

" Oh! But that's queer. What is it short for?

I shall call you Lindy; it fits you. Frost will take your things in; we're going to have tea out here in the sunshine—at once, if you don't mind." And Maidlin plunged into an eager apology as she led them up to the terrace. "I'm expecting other visitors; I'm so sorry they chose the day you were arriving. They won't be able to stay very long; Mrs. Robertson has a dinner engagement to-night. Dr. Robertson asked if he might bring his sister and his nephew to see our Abbey—well, sister-in-law, I suppose! They're all Robertsons. They'd been so very good to me that I didn't want to put them off."

"We'll keep out of your way while you entertain them." Anne took the basket-chair offered her rather wearily. "It's more than kind of you to let us come here, Miss di Ravarati. What a lovely place! Is it your home?" Her eyes rested on the velvet lawn, the old trees just beginning to bud, some almonds and prunus in flower, and the borders of daffodils and narcissus.

"I've lived here for eleven years, since I was fourteen. But, please, you mustn't call me by my long name! I keep that for business purposes."

"Programmes?" Lindy's eyes sparkled. "Oh, Miss—Miss Angel! We heard you sing on Thursday —it was my birthday treat. It was too gorgeous for words!"

Maidlin raised her dark brows. "You were in the Free Trade Hall? I didn't know I was singing to you. I'd been longing to take part in *Gerontius* for ages. It was after the concert that Dr. Robertson asked if they might come to see the Abbey."

"What Abbey? We didn't know there was one."

"Ruins, in our garden." Maidlin was busy with her cups and the teapot. "I'm going to show the Robertsons round; I'll take you later and tell you all the stories. But please don't call me Miss Angel! I've had quite enough teasing already. I'm Maidlin, or Maid; it's a North-country form of Madeline or Magdalene, and I lived in the North as a child."

"Oh, how pretty!" Anne exclaimed. "May we really say Miss Maidlin?"

"It sounds more friendly. As Lindy says, my whole name is for programmes. What is her name short for?" Maidlin carried a cup to Anne.

"Belinda," Lindy said ruefully. "Isn't it terrible? It's one of our family names."

Maidlin stood holding a plate of scones and laughed down at her. "Not Belinda Bellanne? Really? Oh, that's fascinating! You ought to be proud of a name like that."

"In a way I am, but Belinda is frightfully heavy, isn't it?"

"Not if you make it Lindy for ordinary use! I thought your sister's name was charming—Anne Bellanne. But yours is just as nice. How clever of your parents!"

"We're supposed to have had a very beautiful ancestor called Anne, in the fifteenth century," Anne explained. "Somehow the family came to be called by her name."

"*La belle Anne!* I see. And I suppose you always have one girl called Anne, after her?"

Anne assented. "But I'm more often called

Nan. Is that a bit of your ruin, that grey wall behind the trees?"

" That's part of the refectory roof. We can only see it before the leaves come on those beech trees. The Abbey is beautiful, and in a queer way it seems part of our life; you'll understand when you've been in it. How are you, Miss Bellanne? Nancy said you'd had 'flu; you don't look very fit yet. You must rest for the first few days, and you'll soon be all right."

" Do you have this glorious sunshine all the time? A day or two of it will put me right," Anne said wistfully. " It's what I need. We've had such a long winter, and The Grange was so cold."

" You went at the wrong time. In another month the moors will be lovely. We often go to The Grange."

" Oh, I know! We love the moors. But not in snow!"

" I could sunbathe," Lindy said. " Fancy having tea out of doors! We seemed months away from that at home. Do you ever have sunstroke?"

Maidlin rose and went in by the big front door. As her guests watched with startled eyes, she came out again wearing a garden hat of very light straw, with a brim almost the size of a cartwheel. It had a blue ribbon, to suit her frock, and was of golden straw which matched the bold patterns woven into the hem and side panels of her dress. In her hand she carried a pyramid of huge hats in all colours.

" Choose! We keep them for visitors."

Lindy hurled her travelling hat aside. " Oh, a green one, please! What a marvellous idea! Here,

Nan! Bright pink for you! Now we look like a rainbow having tea!"

"Why, what's the matter, Anne Bellanne?" Maidlin spoke with mock severity.

Anne was laughing almost hysterically. "The difference! Do you know what I saw as soon as I reached The Grange? A row of snow-boots and Wellingtons. *They* keep *them* for visitors! And you offer us sun hats!" She threw off her felt and crammed a rose-pink hat on her dark head. "There, Miss Madalena!"

"It suits you," Maidlin said. "The Grange visitors are usually hardy young things who want to tramp the moors in all weathers. Nancy's had to fit them out so often that she keeps a selection of Wellingtons ready. We like to go without hats here, and it isn't really hot enough for these yet, but there are times when the sun just blazes on this terrace, and if you want to bask in it and read or go to sleep, you simply must have either a hat or a headache. People won't go upstairs to fetch proper hats, but they don't mind sticking on one of these, as they're so light to wear and yet so shady."

"And such lovely colours!" Anne added. "Yours matches the pattern on your dress perfectly."

"Your frock's a gorgeous blue," Lindy exclaimed. "How do you get those marvellous gold and orange patterns on it, Miss Maidlin? Are they done by hand?"

"Exactly what I was wanting to ask, but I hadn't the cheek," Anne remarked. "Lindy, you haven't been here half an hour. How can you?"

" Haven't I? Well, I feel that I've been here for a week. Miss Maidlin's made us so much at home with her huge cartwheel hats. And she talked about our names!" Lindy protested.

Maidlin's colour rose. " I do want you to feel at home. My frock's hand-woven, Belinda Bellanne; my best pal has a loom and she wove it for me. There's not another piece in the whole world exactly like mine. Now do please go on with your tea! The other car may arrive at any moment."

" And we ought to be out of the way so that you can attend to them." Anne grasped the situation. " We'll go and unpack."

" And then wander about the garden. The orchard is over there, and the daffodils under the trees are a wonderful sight."

" Is it the man who conducted at the concert? May I peep at him from a window?" Lindy begged.

" Dr. Robertson. Mrs. Robertson—his sister-in-law—took care of me in Manchester; we had to stay the night there, of course. I didn't need to be taken care of in the least," Maidlin smiled, as she poured out second cups of tea. " I'm used to travelling; I go to Italy every year. But Dr. Robertson wouldn't believe that, so he made his sister go to look after me. She was very kind, and it was much jollier to be with a party than to be alone in a strange town."

" Were you nervous?" Lindy's eyes were full of adoration.

" Have another scone! Just a little; I always am. But it goes as soon as I begin to sing; I forget everything but the lovely music. If you go exploring you may meet the family," and Maidlin turned the conversation from herself. "Mary Devine has taken the twins for a picnic, so that I'd have a clear field for all my visitors. Mary is Joy's secretary; Joy is Lady Quellyn, and this is her house, but she's in New York. Mary also writes books for girls, so she's kept busy. The twins are Lady Quellyn's children; some day she'll take them to the States with her, but at present they're left with Mary and me. Next door, at Marchwood Manor, there's a crowd of small cousins—three boys, a girl, and a baby who is another girl. The Grange was their mother's home before she married," and she looked at Anne. " She turned her old house into a holiday hostel and asked Nancy Rowney to take care of her guests."

" It's a lovely idea! I hope you don't think I've been ungrateful about my time there," Anne said anxiously. " I felt the invitation, to a complete stranger, was just too kind for words. It's a beautiful way to use her old home. I didn't mean to criticise. And Miss Rowney was so very kind."

" But you were cold," Maidlin agreed. " You went there too soon after your illness; you weren't ready to be braced up. Oh, I understand! You should have come here to bask in sunshine first; then you'd have been fit for the moors. We all go to The Grange when we want bracing air. Now I think—yes, I hear a car. Do you mind?" She rang a tinkly cowbell, and the maid came to take the cups and plates.

Lindy sprang up. " We'll skip out of sight. But I shall peek at Dr. Robertson from upstairs."

Anne rose hastily. " Thanks for the tea and a lovely rest! I feel better already."

Maidlin was looking at the car which had appeared at the end of the beech avenue. " Yes, it is the Robertsons' car. You'll take Miss Bellanne upstairs, won't you, Edith?"—to the maid.

There was a sudden touch of colour in her face as she went down the terrace steps to greet the new guests, the big golden hat like a halo still on her dark head.

" She wants to see one of them rather extra specially much," Anne said to herself. " Now which is it? The young man or the older one? Not the elderly lady, I think! What a thrill! Lindy hasn't noticed; I'll keep my suspicions to myself, but if The Angel of *Gerontius* isn't a little bit interested in one of those visitors, I'm not Anne Bellanne!"

CHAPTER IV

LINDY FINDS THE ABBEY

" Nan, come and look!" Lindy whispered. " Such a nice man! He and Miss Angel make a lovely couple!"

" Dr. Robertson? Be careful, Lin; and don't stay there and watch. It's rude. Just look at your musician, and then come and help me to unpack."

" I didn't mean Dr. Robertson. He looks much nicer than he does on the platform—quite human and jolly. He's rather stern when he's conducting. But I mean the other man."

" The boy?" Anne glanced out at the group by the car. " He's very good-looking, but he's too young."

" Why shouldn't he be young? He's not a boy!" Lindy protested. " He ought to marry Miss Maid. They look so nice together."

" He's too young for her," Anne repeated, her eyes on the handsome lad, who was obviously chaffing his hostess about her very large hat.

Maidlin, laughing and flushed, whipped it off and tossed it on the grass. She pointed to the pile of garden hats, and he selected a bright blue one and clapped it on his head and laughed down at her. He was tall and fair and sunburnt, and about the same age as Maidlin.

" I bet Miss Angel had forgotten she was still wearing hers!" Lindy laughed. " Doesn't Dr. Robertson look a dear, Nan?"

" He has a kind face, and thoughtful; he looks like a student, and an artist. Now, Lin, that's enough! You've seen him; now come and help me."

Lindy turned from the window reluctantly. But her delight in the two pretty bedrooms, one looking over the lawn and garden, the other on an orchard with a sheen of gold under the bare trees, was so great that she had no time for regrets. Her next glance down at the terrace, when the unpacking was finished, showed that the group round the tea-table had disappeared.

" They've gone into the ruins. I shall go and look at that orchard. Coming, Nan?"

" No, I'll sit here in the sun. We've come a long way to-day." Anne sank into a chintz-covered chair by the window. " How beautiful that lawn is!"

" And this morning we were in Manchester and it was raining!" Lindy sighed ecstatically.

She ran down to the terrace, seized her huge green hat, and raced off towards a gate in a south wall which opened into the orchard. Here were sheets of wild daffodils under bare apple and pear trees, and she stood entranced. On the old walls were peaches and nectarines, covered with deep red blossom.

" What a gorgeous place! It makes me want to dance," and Lindy did a few steps of an Irish jig which she had learnt at school. She curtsied to a budding cherry tree and turned back into the garden.

" I want to see those ruins. I won't disturb Miss

Maid, if she's still there. I wonder if this little path is the way she went?"

The narrow track between bushes led to an ancient gate, studded with great nails and crossed by bars of iron. It was ajar, so Belinda pushed it open and stood gazing at a tiny garden, gay with brown and golden wallflower. Looking down on the carpet of flowers was a high grey wall, with wide windows which appeared to be very old. The path led through the garden to an arched doorway, and Lindy tiptoed down a dark tunnelled passage towards a gleam of sunlit grass.

" Oh, what a marvellous place!" She gazed about at a small square lawn, very green, and enclosed by grey walls. Low doorways with sharply-pointed arches seemed to lead to rooms inside the walls; on one side there was a sort of arcade with a covered walk—the remains of the cloisters, but Lindy did not know that. One wall, opposite where she stood, had a great gap in it, and what seemed to be a field lay beyond.

" Nan will love this," Lindy thought. " The orchard made me want to dance; perhaps because all those flowers were dancing! But here I feel like being in church. There's a holy sort of spell about it. I suppose it was a holy place long ago. I'd like to sing! But those people are somewhere about. Oh, horrors, here they come! I promised to keep out of the way!"

At the sound of voices, and Maidlin's deep happy laugh, Lindy shot into the nearest doorway in panic. It proved to be the beginning of a stone staircase with wide uneven steps; she darted up and found

herself in a long light room, all of stone except the
oak roof.

On one side there was a row of window-slits, each
reached by a step. She climbed into the first and
looked out, and found the green garth below her.
Maidlin and her party had come from a doorway
close to the entrance to the stair which Lindy had
found; they stood talking on the lawn and then
crossed to another ancient door, below wide beautiful windows, and went out of her sight.

"Those people do look nice!" Lindy leaned
from her window to survey the Abbey from this
vantage-point. "The young man's awfully handsome, and anybody can see he admires Miss Angel
by the way he looks at her. Dr. Robertson looks
kinder and less alarming every time I see him. His
face is terribly nice when he laughs. I'd better not
stay; they may come up here next and I'd be
caught. There's no way out of this big room except
by the steps, unless I leap out of one of the windows." She crept very carefully to the unfenced
openings at the end of the dormitory, and drew
back hastily. "No, thanks! Too many stones
down there. I'll come back and explore another
time, when I won't interfere with Miss Maid. It's
a lovely old place. Fancy having it as part of your
garden!"

She slipped unseen into the tunnel again and back
through the wallflower-garden to the lawn. Waving
her hand to Anne at her window, she wandered
down another winding path through a shrubbery.

"I don't suppose it leads to more ruins, but it
must go somewhere. Here's a gate, and a lane,

and gate number two on the other side. Does it all belong to Lady Quellyn, I wonder?"

She leaned on the gate, looking at a stretch of parkland and a small lake, with an islet which held one big tree. Beyond were bare orchard trees, reached by a gate in a fence.

"I think it's a different house. Didn't Miss Maid say something about next door? *What's that?*"

It was a shriek of terror; there was no doubt of that. Another shriek—a scream of rage—an urgent call for assistance. "Help! Oh, help!"

Lindy looked round wildly. Then she dashed across the grass, past the lake, and towards a clump of trees, from which those agonised shrieks came steadily.

A woman was struggling with a red-haired girl of almost nine, who was fighting to get away from her. From a tree above them came another wild scream, and the child fought more fiercely than ever. "Let me go! Must help Marg'ret!"

"Get me down! Get me down! I'm stuck!" wailed someone in the tree.

Lindy rushed to help. "Can I do anything? What's the matter with this one?"

"Want to get Twin down," sobbed the child on the ground.

"She'll dash up into the tree and then there will be two to rescue," Mary Devine panted. "Elizabeth, if you'll wait here I'll try to get Margaret down."

"She's stuck! She'll be there for always! Let me go, Mary!" Elizabeth's struggles grew more frantic.

Lindy grasped the situation. " What a little ass you are!" she said frankly. " Is she called Elizabeth? Hang on to her! She'll only make more trouble. I'll try to help the other one. Where is she?"

" Twin's stuck in that beashly tree. And I'm not a little ass," Elizabeth sobbed.

" You're just a silly baby," Lindy retorted. " Is Number Two called Margaret? Hi, Margaret! Where are you?"

" Here!" Margaret wailed. " And I can't get down. It was easy coming up! It's a beashly tree, like Twin said." A tear-stained face in a mop of dark-red curls peered down at Lindy.

" Gosh! You are in a pickle! How am I going to get at you?" Lindy exclaimed. " I say, kid, keep still—quite still! Don't wriggle or try to come down. That branch doesn't like having a thing as big as you on it. Don't bring it down or you'll come down with it."

" Want to come down!"

" I want Twin to come down!" Elizabeth shouted.

" Yes, but not that way," Lindy said sharply. " Keep still, Margaret!"

The branch was rotten and was bending under Margaret's weight. A fall from that height might have serious consequences. Margaret, in a reckless fit, had run on ahead and had climbed the trunk without difficulty, because her boy cousins had said girls could not climb; she knew Elizabeth could be trusted to give a vivid account of her triumph to Andrew and Tony. She had wormed her way along a branch, which had grown suddenly slim and had begun to sway dangerously. Margaret had lost her nerve and screamed for help, clinging to the bough with arms and knees, and Elizabeth's one thought had been to rush up the tree after her.

Lindy eyed Margaret's position with some alarm. The weight of another person would certainly bring down the branch. But could the child be trusted to keep still until help could be fetched? Certainly not with Elizabeth in this distraught condition just below her.

" Elizabeth, you've heard of kittens climbing trees and needing to be brought down?" Lindy spoke quietly. " Well, your Margaret is the kitten up the tree. We need a ladder, and a man; you always need ladders and men when there's a kitten up a tree. Sometimes the fire-engine has to come. Couldn't you run to the house and bring a man and a ladder? Which house is nearest?"

" Home!" Elizabeth shouted, and shot off through the park to the little gate and the lane.

" Fetch Frost, Elizabeth!" Mary Devine called after her. " She's right, though she didn't stop to think," she added. " It would take longer to go to the Manor, and Sir Kenneth is out, I know."

" It will be easier now she's gone." Lindy looked up into the tree again. " Margaret, play at being the kitten in the tree. Cling to that branch with your claws and don't move; you're too frightened to move, you know. You can call ' Meaow ' if you like."

Realistic and terrified cat-wails came from Margaret. " Is that right?" she asked anxiously.

" I'd like Twin to hear me. I won't really fall off, will I?"

" Not if you keep still and hold on like a kitten." Lindy turned to Mary. " She's the wrong way round. If I climb up I'll only be able to grab her feet, and she can't possibly turn without falling off. If she'll keep still I think she'll be all right. Don't move, kitten! Meaow some more to call the fire-engine!"

" Oh, it's going to break!" Mary cried in terror.

The branch had given an ominous crack, and Margaret's meaow became a shriek once more.

Lindy leapt for the tree, hurled herself up the trunk, and crept along a stout branch, just below the one to which the child was clinging. She had had her eye on it for some moments.

" I may break her fall anyway," she muttered. " Hope she doesn't break my neck at the same time!"

The rotten branch gave way with a crash. Lindy braced herself for the shock.

Margaret, with a wild scream, hurtled down upon her. Lindy flung out one arm, clinging to her bough with the other. She caught Margaret by the shoulder and was dragged from her perch by the sudden strain. They crashed to the ground together, Lindy underneath.

With a shout two men came rushing from the direction of the Hall. The younger, running like the wind, reached the group first.

" What's the row? Can I help? Are they hurt?" he cried.

CHAPTER V

THE KITTEN IN THE TREE

ELIZABETH, rushing frantically to the garage, ran into the party returning from the Abbey. Exhausted, she fell at their feet, gasping out her story.

" Twin's a kitten in a tree—she can't get down —a girl said men must come—or the fire-engine— oh, Aunty Maid! Get Twin out of that beashly tree!"

" Tree? Fire-engine? Kitten? Elizabeth, what's the matter? Where's Margaret?" Maidlin cried.

" I told you—in a tree. We can't get her down."

" Who is in trouble?" asked Dr. Robertson. " Can't we help?"

" The other twin. Where is she, Elizabeth?"

" Near the lake. A girl came—and she said, bring a ladder," Elizabeth wailed.

" Down that path," Maidlin said breathlessly to her guests. " Oh, do you mind? You'll see the gate, and the lake's in the park across the lane. I'll fetch Frost and a ladder," and she ran to the garage.

Elizabeth stumbled to her feet and raced after the men, who had set off down the shrubbery path. The lady who had been with them followed, but more slowly.

As young Donald Robertson rushed to the group under the trees, Margaret picked herself up and began to dance and shout. " I'm down! I'm out

of the beashly tree! Thought I'd never get down
again! I was the kitten up the tree! We didn't
need the fire-engine! Oh, I say! Did I bash that
nice girl when I tumbled on her?'' She sobered
suddenly.

A glance had shown Mary that the twin was un-
hurt and she was bending over Belinda anxiously.
Lindy had not moved, and Mary looked up in distress at the two men.

'' She fell from that branch. Could you help me
to carry her to the house?''

Margaret, in an agony of remorse, flung herself
on Lindy, sobbing brokenly. '' I did it! I tumbled
on her—I knocked her out of that beashly tree!
Is she killed? Oh, make her get up and talk to us!
I never meant to hit her—I never did!''

The elder man was examining the limp body with
capable, sensitive hands. '' She's had a nasty fall.
Could we take her to the hospital? Don, run to
meet Miss Maidlin and tell her we don't need the
ladder but we do want some sort of stretcher. This
child must be lifted carefully; there may be internal
injury. Don! Tell Miss Maid gently! Don't give
her a shock—more than she's had already.''

'' Trust me. She was so happy this afternoon,
poor kid!'' he muttered as he ran. '' That little
brat! What was she doing up in the tree?''

He met Elizabeth, panting and exhausted, and
stopped to say a word of warning. Small girls were
unknown creatures to him, but he guessed that
these two were to blame for the accident, and he
did not love them for bringing a pleasant afternoon
to a tragic end.

" Now, see here, you young monkey! Your sister's all right, but the other girl is badly hurt. Don't go howling round and making matters worse. You've done quite enough harm already."

Elizabeth stared after him in blazing wrath, as he ran to meet Maidlin. " Don't like that man! I never did no harm at all. I only tried to help Twin. And I'm not howling round. He's a pig." She raced on to the scene of the accident.

Donald Robertson, his sympathy in his eyes, looked down into Maidlin's frightened face. " Miss Maidlin, your second twin is all right, but the other girl is hurt. My uncle wants a stretcher instead of the ladder."

Maidlin, white and shaken, caught at his arm to steady herself. " Will you tell Frost? Tell him to bring a deck-chair—it makes quite a good stretcher—and some rugs. Give me one minute! Is it little Belinda?"

" I've no idea. A fair-haired girl, much older than your twins."

" How shall I tell her sister?" Maidlin groaned. " They only arrived at tea-time! Oh, our twins! They ought to be locked up till they're seventeen!"

" Now that's a rattling good idea!" Donald said with enthusiasm. " What about boarding-school?"

But Maidlin was hurrying on to see for herself what had happened. " No, don't come, please. I'm all right. If you would—it would help me so much—if you'd explain to your mother what has happened, and send Frost after me, that would be all the help in the world. I don't know what Mrs. Robertson will think of us!''

'' Blest if I know what's happened!'' Donald gazed after her slight figure as she ran. Then he turned to speak to Frost and to stop his mother from joining the crowd round Lindy.

'' Uncle's there and you know what a capable old boy he is. And there was a governess or somebody with the kids, so she'll stand by Miss Maidlin.''

'' A pity she couldn't take better care of the children,'' Mrs. Robertson said severely.

'' Oh, I don't know! Two like that must be rather a handful. I wouldn't like her job; I should send 'em to school.''

'' No, you wouldn't; not if their mother was in New York,'' Mrs. Robertson said tartly.

'' She should take them with her. Why should Miss Maidlin be worried like this?''

His mother glanced at him sharply. '' You seem very much concerned about Miss Maidlin!''

'' Well, who wouldn't be? She had a fearful shock, and she feels things a lot or she couldn't sing as she does.''

'' Oh, of course! She's an artist and very sensitive. But——'' Mrs. Robertson did not speak her thought aloud, but glanced doubtfully at her tall son. '' I shall go back to the car,'' she said. '' It will only worry them to have us about, and we must get away soon. We have that engagement, you know.''

'' I'll see if I can do anything,'' and Donald turned back towards the lake again. '' I'll remind

Uncle he must get back to town, but if I could be any use here I'll stay."

Mrs. Robertson returned to the car, looking thoughtful. As she reached it Anne came from the house to meet her.

" Oh, please excuse me! But do you know what has happened? I heard screams and then everybody disappeared. Has there been an accident?"

" I believe so, but not to one of the Quellyn twins; I understand it is an older girl who has been hurt."

Then Mrs. Robertson was left, staring blankly, as Anne rushed off in the direction taken by all the rest, with a cry that sounded like " Lindy!"

Half asleep by the window in the sunshine, she had watched Maidlin and the visitors come from the Abbey path, had seen Elizabeth's stormy entrance and the exit of Maidlin and the men, and had hurried down to find out what had happened. An accident to one of the children seemed the probable explanation; she had never dreamt of harm coming to Belinda.

She caught Frost, laden with a deck-chair, and recognised him as the man who had met them at the station. " Oh, do you know what has happened?" she begged.

" Miss Maidlin wanted a ladder, to fetch one of the children out of a tree." Frost was hurrying down the path. " Then she sent word it was to be a stretcher, and a chair would do. I hope Miss Margaret hasn't fallen and hurt herself; it would be Miss Margaret. Miss Elizabeth takes more care."

" No, it isn't one of them. I'm afraid it's my

little sister." Anne caught her breath. " I expect she tried to help. It's hard lines if she's been hurt," she said unsteadily.

" We'll see in two ticks." Frost's voice was gruff with sympathy. " Those children are always in a pickle."

Maidlin saw them coming. Kneeling by Lindy, she had kept one eye on the path. Springing up, she said breathlessly to Dr. Robertson: " I know you'll lift her carefully. Frost will help you; he's very gentle. I can't do any more here; cover her up well, you know. I must speak to her sister."

She ran across the grass. " Oh, Miss Bellanne— Anne! Oh, I am so sorry, my dear. I don't know yet how it happened."

" Is she badly hurt?" Anne asked shakily.

" I don't know. We'll have the doctor at once. Come back with me and we'll phone for him. You can't do anything for Lindy," Maidlin pleaded, " and it will only make you feel worse to go and look at her. Dr. Robertson knows what to do; I could see that by the way he examined her; and he's very careful. He and Frost will bring her to the house. We'll help most by sending for the doctor."

" Do you know what happened?" Anne's voice shook.

" Mary Devine tried to tell me. She feels it was her fault, but that's nonsense. Margaret ran away from her and climbed the tree." Maidlin described the accident so far as she understood it. " It was terribly plucky of your Lindy. She must have known she might be hurt; Mary heard her say to

herself that she hoped Margaret wouldn't break
her neck when she fell on her. Lindy saw what
might happen, but she tried to catch Margaret, or
at least to break her fall. It was very brave. You
must be proud of her."

" If only she isn't——!" Anne began.

" Oh, I'm sure she isn't! Dr. Robertson didn't
look like that," Maidlin cried. " But we may have
to take care of her for a while; I expect there's
slight concussion. I hope it's no worse than that."

" I must go to her," Anne said brokenly.

" I can't help you, then," Maidlin retorted, badly
overwrought. " I'm going to ring up the doctor.
That really will help Lindy. Staring at her is no
use!" And she ran on, leaving Anne hesitating.

Drawn to Belinda by every bit of her nature, she
turned to hurry towards the lake. But it had all
been too much, and she could do no more. Suddenly everything went dark; she leaned against
the gate and then slid to the ground, and lay in the
path the stretcher-bearers must take.

" Gosh!" The twins, running ahead, stood staring down at her. " Here's somebody else! She's
dead."

" Let's call somebody to do something," Margaret suggested vaguely.

Elizabeth rushed back along the track and
caught Mary's hand. " There's a lady, and she's
dead, near the gate! Come and look at her!"

" What's that?" Dr. Robertson had been walking by the stretcher, which was borne by Frost and
Donald.

" Come and look!" Elizabeth caught his hand and Mary's and dragged them on ahead.

" Fainted.   She'll be all right in a moment. We'll leave her to you." He looked at Mary. " We must get the child to the house. There's something wrong with her shoulder; perhaps the collar-bone has gone. The doctor will have to set it. Will you take charge here? Is this a sister of our patient?"

" I think so. But I haven't seen her before. I'll stay here till she comes round."

Dr. Robertson nodded and followed the stretcher-bearers towards the house.

Anne came back to life to find three anxious faces bending over her, two of them framed in dark-red curls and with frightened brown eyes.

" Thought you were dead!" broke from one twin.

" You did give us a beashly fright," the other said reproachfully.

" Let me help you to the house.   We don't think your sister is badly hurt, but it must have been a horrible shock for you," Mary Devine said.

Anne sat up and rested her head on her hands. " Did I go off? Oh, I am sorry! I've given you more trouble. Miss Maidlin told me to go with her, but I wanted so much to see Lindy. Can you tell me how she is?"

" Dr. Robertson is sure she'll be all right. Don't be frightened about her, please! He was very re-assuring and emphatic. But she has hurt one shoulder; the doctor will put that right."

" I tumbled on her. It was me that did it," the younger twin said remorsefully.

" Margaret fell, and your sister tried to catch her. Her right shoulder must have had a fearful wrench with the sudden strain. But she saved Margaret from a terrible fall."

" Twin might have been in pieces," Elizabeth said. " What's the nice girl's name?"

" Lindy. And I'm Nan. I'm so sorry to have been a nuisance." Anne looked up at Mary. " But it was so sudden, and after the journey—I was very tired."

" And you still aren't fit after your illness. The shock was too much for you. It's we who are sorry," Mary said earnestly. " We've given you and your sister a horrid welcome to the Abbey."

" We had a beautiful welcome from Miss Maidlin. I'm glad Lindy was able to help."

" She helped an awful lot." Elizabeth seized Anne's hand, gazing into her face. " She helped Twin, who was in a gashly mess up in that tree."

" Said I was a kitten in the beashly tree," Margaret added. " What does Lindy mean? It's a funny name."

" Let us help you to the house, Miss Bellanne," Mary suggested.

" It means Belinda. She's Belinda Bellanne." Anne rose stiffly and clung to Mary for a moment. " Thanks! I'll be all right now. It was silly of me."

" Belinda Bellanne!" Elizabeth gave a chuckle of delight. " I shan't call her all that! I shall say just Belinn Bellanne! That's a lovely name!"

" It's something nobody else has ever called her, anyway," Anne said.

" I think Billy should be her name; Billy Bell-anne," Margaret suggested.

" Original minds! Very good ideas too," Anne agreed. " You must tell Lindy yourselves when she's better." Her lips pinched for a moment. " Shall we go to the house? I'm all right now."

" Are you bothered about Belinn Bellanne?" Elizabeth took her hand and walked sedately by her side.

" About Billy Bellanne!" Margaret shouted.

" A little bothered. Suppose we try to be very quiet in case she's asleep."

" We'll creep into the house like mice," said Mary.

" Or kittens," Elizabeth added. " We'll all be kittens, just come down out of trees. Then we shan't wake Belinn-Billy."

" Oh, make it Billy-Belinn!" Anne begged, half laughing.

CHAPTER VI

MARCHWOOD TWINS

THE doctor's report was good. Lindy's collar-bone was not broken; the shoulder-joint was wrenched out of place, but that was put right quickly; she woke from unconsciousness, gave Anne a brief grin, and fell asleep.

"She'll do. Let her sleep it off. Any other patients for me? Shall I have a look at Margaret?" asked the doctor, who had known the twins for the whole of their eight years and eleven months. Like Frost he added: "It would be Margaret, of course. All right this time? And you, my dear?" to Maidlin. "Not suffering from shock?"

"Not seriously, Doctor. But you might look at Lindy's sister. She had a much worse shock."

"We can't have our Angel knocked up," he said. "Oh yes, I heard you sing, child. I congratulate you on another big success. Now where is this sister?"

"I shall be all right, if you're sure Lindy isn't really hurt," Anne protested, as he questioned her. He drew from her the whole story—the 'flu, the cold holiday on the moors, the journey from the north only that morning, the shock and suspense of the accident, and the moment of faintness by the gate, of which she was much ashamed—and gave his verdict promptly. "A day or two in bed for both of you. Your sister's all right; no need to worry. You've come to a good place; Miss Mary and Miss Maid will take care of you—I know them! Ring me up if anything goes wrong, Madalena; but it won't. These two aren't patients—not real casualties. They need a rest-cure, that's all. Get to bed and stay there for the week-end,'' he commanded Anne.

She heard his car drive away, and then, resting in a big chair, could not help hearing voices just below her window.

'' I shall stay for an hour or two, to see if there is anything I can do.'' That was Dr. Robertson's deep musical bass.

'' But, Jock, what about that dinner?'' Mrs. Robertson urged.

'' Uncle Jock, I'll stay; I'd love to! You take Mother to the dinner!'' Donald said eagerly.

'' Don't be absurd, boy. You'll escort your mother, of course. The people are her friends, and they want to hear about your visit to the Cape. You can make my apologies. I'll come home later by train.''

'' Oh, but, Uncle Jock——!'' Donald began.

'' Nonsense!'' The door slammed and the car drove away—with Donald still protesting, no doubt.

Anne laughed wearily. '' Did Dr. Robertson put him into the car by force? Odd to think of such a great man as ' Jock '! I must tell Lindy; she calls him Dr. John Robertson. He knows how to get his own way. That boy wanted to stay and help—oh, why don't they remember windows may be open?''

" You're more than kind, but there wasn't the slightest need for anybody to stay." It was Maidlin's clear contralto voice.

Anne dived for her bed and pulled a pillow over her head. To bang the window shut would have startled those below.

A hand on her shoulder made her look up, and she found Mary beside her, gazing at her anxiously.

" Oh, good! I was afraid you were weeping!" Mary exclaimed. " You gave me quite a fright!"

" I was trying not to listen to people who would talk just under my window!" Anne retorted. " Have they gone? It was Miss Maidlin and one of her visitors."

" They're walking on the lawn. Maid thinks a great deal of Dr. Robertson. She has sung for him several times," Mary said sedately.

Anne gave her a quick look. Was there perhaps just a touch of reserve in her manner? Did the secretary suspect that Miss Maidlin's feeling for her conductor was not entirely musical? Still more important, did Miss Maid herself suspect it? On the whole, Anne thought she did not, but she did not yet know Madalena well enough to feel sure.

" I came to see if I could help you to bed. I want to bring you up some supper, so that you can go to sleep." Mary changed the subject firmly.

Anne postponed all that she would have liked to say. The events of the afternoon had flung herself and Lindy into a closer relationship with those in the house than would have happened in several days of ordinary acquaintance, but she had not yet reached a point when she could ask questions about very private affairs.

" We're giving you a terrible lot of trouble," she said. " Oh, I don't need help, thanks very much! Bed is a pleasant idea, and I'd love to rest and go to sleep, but it feels so rude. We're guests, and we've only just arrived, though it seems a long time ago."

" Doctor's orders," Mary smiled. " Of course you must go to bed. And please do remember how grateful we are to your sister for the way she came rushing to help, and for her courage too—for she knew there was a big risk to herself in breaking Margaret's fall as she did. We feel we have given trouble to you, not the other way round. You must let us try to make up for it. It has spoiled the start of your visit; we'll do our best to make the rest of your time pleasanter. I'll go and see about your supper."

A long night's rest did wonders for Anne. She slept on and on, not knowing how often Maidlin or Mary looked in to see if she was awake. She turned over at last, glanced at her watch, and sprang out of bed.

" Eleven o'clock! What is the matter with me? And where am I? I must have been dead asleep." Her eyes swept round the unfamiliar pretty room and found the sunlit garden through the open window. " Oh, the beautiful place! And—Lindy!" as the events of the evening came back to her.

She flung her dressing-gown round her shoulders

and ran to the next room. At the door she checked herself and stood staring, and then laughed.

A twin in a green frock sat on each side of Belinda, who lay, bright-eyed and eager, gazing at them in turn. Elizabeth held up a warning finger to Anne.

" She's not to talk. She mustn't get excited. We were being quiet because you were asleep."

" We're doing the talking!" Margaret announced. " We're going to give her her breakfast as soon as it's ready."

" You bet you are!—and doing the talking too!" Lindy chuckled. " Are you all right, Nan? I'm O.K. I say, they're priceless kids!"

" We've told her about being Belinn and Billy. She doesn't mind. And Margaret's said she's sorry."

" But *I* mind!" Anne said promptly. " I'd rather have her called Lindy. It's a nice name."

" We'll call her Aunt Lindy sometimes," Elizabeth conceded.

" I shall call her Aunty Lin!" Margaret shouted.

" Do you know them apart, Nan?" Lindy grinned. " I do, as soon as they speak. Margaret always shrieks."

" I don't! Oh, Aunt Lindy, I don't!"

" Well, you're doing it now," Elizabeth observed, and looked up at Anne. " Do we call you Aunt Lindy's sister? Or are you something else?"

" She said she was something else last night, silly."

" I said I was called Nan." Anne sat on the

bed. "We haven't been introduced, but I know you're the Quellyn twins and one of you is Margaret."

"Oh no!" The twins spoke together in shocked reproof. "We aren't Quellyn twins. People call us that, but we're not."

"We're Marchwood twins," Margaret added. "Fancy not knowing that, when you've come to stay in our house! I'm Margaret Joan Marchwood. Twin's Elizabeth Joy Marchwood."

"Did you ever hear before of girls having a different name from their mother?" Elizabeth asked. "For we have, you know. Mother used to be called Marchwood, like us, but now she's Lady Quellyn, and our little brother is David Quellyn."

"He's only half a little brother!" Margaret shouted.

"Half a—oh, a little stepbrother. I see," Anne said, laughing.

"I don't like it very much," Elizabeth said wistfully. "We ought to be called the same as Mother. We thought we'd turn into Quellyn too when she did; but she said we couldn't do that. Elizabeth Quellyn would sound fearfully funny, wouldn't it?"

"No funnier than Margaret Quellyn. I'd rather be called Marchwood."

"Well, you are, and you will be, so you needn't worry," Elizabeth crushed her. "But it is odd, isn't it, Miss Nan?"

"I suppose it is, but you must be used to it by now."

"Andrew and Tony and Rosemary, at the

Manor, are called Marchwood too," Elizabeth remarked.

" And Michael and Katharine—she's the baby,"
Margaret added.

" You're well off for cousins. I haven't any,"
Lindy said.

" Well, stay here and we'll let you see ours sometimes," Elizabeth said kindly. " You'll stay for a
long while, won't you? We like you, because you
told Margaret about being a kitten in a tree."

" It was a beashly horrid tree," Margaret said
viciously.

" I think I'd better stay altogether, to take care
of the two of you," Lindy mocked. " You need a
keeper. And I need a job."

" Not at all a bad idea." Maidlin came in with
a tray. " Good-morning, Miss Bellanne; you look
much better, and I know you've slept well. You
shall have some breakfast too; Mary will bring it
here and you'll have it with Lindy. Then I think
you should go back to bed as the doctor ordered.
If you both have a quiet day you'll be much more
fit by to-morrow."

" But the sunshine's so lovely," Anne pleaded.
" Couldn't I dress and sit in it, on that delightful
terrace?"

" I want her to see your ruins," Lindy said.
" I had one peep yesterday, but you were busy with
those people, so I came away. I want to see it all,
and Nan will love it."

" Soon," Maidlin said firmly. " You're not
going to move to-day. We're all going to rest. I
shall send the twinnies to the Manor, so that they

can't chatter. As a rule we all go to church on Sundays," and she looked at Anne, while she arranged Lindy's tray. " But with measles in the village that's out of bounds. The children haven't had it, and while their mother's so far away I can't take any risks. So they'll spend the day with their cousins at the Manor, and this house will be very quiet."

" So long as the Robertsons don't ring up every hour to ask how we are," Mary Devine said, bringing a tray for Anne.

Maidlin laughed, a heart-whole, unconscious laugh which answered one of Anne's questions. " They're too silly! They seem terribly upset about you, Lindy. Donald rang up quite early to ask if there was anything he could do, if he came down here on his motor-bike. I begged him not to think of it, of course. And then Dr. Robertson rang, an hour later, to ask how we all were; he didn't know about Donald, so he apologised for disturbing us again. It's very kind and thoughtful, but I do hope they won't go on ringing up all day!"

" If she's interested in either of those men she doesn't know it," Anne said to herself.

" To-morrow," Maidlin went on, " I shall go to Kentisbury, and I shall take the twins with me. That will give you another peaceful day. You can wander in the Abbey; I'll tell you all the stories later on. Almost every stone in it has a story! After two quiet days I should think you'll both be all right."

" Will Tansy be at the Castle?" Margaret looked up quickly.

"She may not have come home from school yet. But you needn't go in the Park; we'll stay with Aunty Ros, and you'll play with Roddy and see Geoffrey-Hugh." Maidlin turned to Anne. "My best friend is married to the Earl of Kentisbury and she has just had her first baby. Hugh was born about two months ago. I go to spend a day at the Castle whenever I can."

"The best friend who made your pretty frock?" Lindy asked. "Or have you lots of them?"

"The same one." Maidlin smiled. "I've only one friend like Rosamund."

"So long as we don't go in the Park," Elizabeth began doubtfully. "Couldn't go in the Park without Tansy. She's awful brave!"

"They had a fright with the deer last autumn," Maidlin explained. "The deer are quite quiet at this time of year, Twinnies; they're too busy with their babies to bother about chasing girls. If you went in the Park you wouldn't even see them; they hide in the lonely parts where you wouldn't go. You mustn't be silly and go on being frightened; it bothers Aunty Ros. But you won't have time for the Park to-morrow. Run along to Nelly and tell her you're going to the Manor for the day."

"Good-bye, Aunty Nan!" said Elizabeth. "Good-bye, Aunty Belinn!"

"Go to sleep for all day, Aunty Billy!" shouted Margaret. "We're going to tell Andy about me being a kitten in a beashly tree!" and she rushed away.

CHAPTER VII

MAIDLIN SHOWS THE ABBEY

MAIDLIN turned to her guests again. " You don't mind their noise, do you? Now, Miss Bellanne, you've heard my programme for you, and I hope you'll agree to it. Two quiet days and then you'll be all right."

" Oh, I'm sure we shall! You're more than kind!"

" But you could be kinder still, Miss Angel!" Lindy hinted, her voice dropping almost to a whisper in her eagerness.

" You really mustn't!" Maidlin cried. " I shall be sorry I sang in Manchester if I'm to go through life as The Angel!"

" Lindy, how can you? What do you mean?" Anne cried.

" Miss Maidlin knows." Lindy's eyes were fixed adoringly on her Angel.

Maidlin stood looking down at her, a smile in the depths of her dark eyes. " How could I be kinder? What have I left undone that I ought to have done?"

" You must practise sometimes. May we listen? And would you—oh, would you sing bits of The Angel again?"

" I never mind singing. We'll have music at night, if you like. I'm working up *Elijah* for the Albert Hall in a few days; you'll be tired of ' O Rest in the Lord ' before the time comes."

" Oh, we shan't! I've heard *Elijah*. You have to be an Angel again, don't you?"

" It's too bad!" Maidlin smiled. " Why shouldn't angels sometimes be sopranos? Yes, it is Angel music, but don't go on calling me Miss Angel, please!"

" It's tempting, but I'll try not to do it! Is it for Dr. Robertson again?"

" He's conducting," Maidlin assented. " He's rather taken me on since Ivor went to New York. He advises me about what concerts to accept and what to sing; I'm asked a good deal now, but I can't take on too much. It's a help to have some-one so experienced to tell me what to do when Joy and Ivor are so far away."

" If she's interested in her conductor, apart from music, she hasn't wakened up to it yet." Anne had watched and listened with interest. " Is it the other one she likes? He seemed a boy beside her. I shouldn't have thought she'd be satisfied with any one so young."

" Nan!" Lindy called urgently, when Maidlin had gone, telling them to rest. " Nan, I want you!"

Anne came from her room. " What is it, Lindy? We must rest, to satisfy these kind people."

" I know. I'm going to sleep again, but I can't till I've asked you something."

" Carry on, then. But don't gossip about your hostess."

" Gossip?" Lindy's eyes widened. " What is there to gossip about? She's lovely, of course, and the kiddies are pets. But this is about me. Nan, you won't tell Miss Maid? I'd die if you did."

Anne sat on the bed and gazed at her. " I should have thought Miss Maidlin was the first person you'd want to tell. I know you asked me in the train not to say a word about your ambition to be a singer, but now that you've met her, why don't you want her to know? She might be able to tell you how to start."

Lindy was scarlet. " I'd feel such a fool. Her voice is so perfect. It would seem awful cheek to think I could ever sing in public! Promise, Nan! Don't tell her! I couldn't bear it!"

" Oh, I'll promise! It's your business, but I think it's a mistake. I'm sure she'd understand, and she'd help you. But it's for you to tell her, when you feel ready to do it, Lin."

" Not yet. If she laughed I should die. I care too much, both about being a singer and about her."

" She wouldn't laugh," Anne said. " You'll give yourself away as soon as you're up again. You always go about singing."

" I'll stop myself. I won't do it here," Lindy said resolutely, and she turned round to go to sleep.

The two days' rest did what the doctor had hoped, and by Monday afternoon both Anne and Lindy were clamouring to be allowed to get up. Maidlin, back from her visit to Kentisbury Castle, agreed that a few hours out of bed might help them to sleep better, and suggested that they should dress and go into the garden.

"Into the Abbey!" Lindy pleaded. "Nan must see it, Miss Angel!"

"We'll show her the Abbey," Elizabeth said firmly. "I'll tell her about Twin falling down the well."

"You're not to! You shan't!" Margaret shouted. "I shall tell her about you being a girl-hero and going in the dark to find rugs for me."

"Silly girl! I shall tell about Aunty Benedicta catching you when you were rushing to fall out of the window."

"Well, I didn't do it!"

"No, but Aunty Benneyben did. Will you stay here and play with us every day?" Elizabeth perched on the bed and gazed into Lindy's face.

"Nothing I'd like better!" Belinda said gaily.

"We've had lots of aunties come, but they all go away again. We'd like you to stay for a long time," said Margaret. "Aunty Gail came, but she didn't stay; and Aunty Benedicta went away too."

"You might add that Aunty Gail burnt her hand saving Elizabeth from a fire, and Aunt Benneyben hurt her head and her arm saving you from a bad fall, Margaret Marchwood," Maidlin said severely. "Then Aunt Lindy comes and hurts her shoulder, helping you out of a tree. I shouldn't think she'd want to stay with such dangerous people."

"We aren't that! We're not!" Margaret cried. "We didn't mean those things to happen!"

"That's why we want her to stay and play games with me and Twin. Things wouldn't happen if she was with us all the time," Elizabeth explained gently.

"Run away now and let Aunt Lindy dress," Maidlin commanded. "Can you manage, Lindy? How does your shoulder feel?"

"Only a little stiff. I'll be all right. I say, you will let me help you with those kids while we're here, won't you?" Lindy offered eagerly, as the twins disappeared. "I'd see they didn't make asses of themselves. I'd look after them for you."

Maidlin gave her a thoughtful look. "That's really very kind, Belinda Bellanne, and we'll be grateful if you will. Mary has rather a big bit of work on hand at present; the proofs of her autumn book came this morning and she ought to get on with them. The twins have a nurse, of course, but they're really too much for her. You'd be a very great help to me. We'll think about it."

Half an hour later Maidlin led Anne and Lindy into the Abbey and told its story, showing chapter-house, refectory, the day-room of the monks and their dormitory, which Lindy found was the long white room she had already seen. They saw the kitchen, under the refectory, the punishment cells, and the sacristy; the site of the great church, where the grass among the fallen stones was carpeted with white violets, and the place where the infirmary or hospital had been. There were many stories, not only of monks and not only legends, but true stories of modern days: of the exploration and discovery of the undreamt-of tunnels and passages and the beautiful little old church underground; of the twins in danger at more than one spot, because of Margaret's carelessness or Elizabeth's mad pranks.

Then Maidlin suggested that Lindy should go

round again with the children to hear their version of these events, and brought cushions for herself and Anne, and spread them on the grass by the door of the chapter-house in the evening sunshine.

" Come and see the parlour, Aunty Belinn!" Elizabeth begged.

" I forgot the parlour!" Maidlin said. " In there, Lindy, that dark little room. There's nothing to see."

" No, but it matters a lot," Margaret said earnestly. " Aunt Billy, it was the only place where the monks could talk; in that one little room. Wasn't that just dreadful for them?"

" That's what the name means," Elizabeth explained. " The parlour is where you talk. Did you know that?"

" I certainly didn't!" Lindy laughed. " But ' parler '—yes, it could be that, I suppose."

" It was that," Margaret retorted. " It was the talking-room. I'd have stayed there all the time."

" I bet you would! Did they really only talk in this dark little place, Miss Angel?"

" We call it the place to tell secrets in," Elizabeth remarked.

" They were silent monks. I expect if they talked in other places it was on business or on holy topics," Maidlin agreed. " For exercise they used to pace up and down the cloisters in silent meditation, and at meals they had sermons read to them. Probably in the ' parlour ' they were allowed to talk freely."

" Gosh! I'm glad I didn't live then!" said Lindy.

" They were all men. You'd have had to find a
nunnery." Maidlin smiled. " Show Aunt Lindy
where your mother used to live, Twinnies."

" Come on!" and the twins raced across the
garth to the cloisters.

Maidlin turned to Anne. " Is Belinda in earnest
when she says she'd like to stay here? Isn't she
going back to school?"

To her surprise a shadow fell on Anne Bellanne's
bright face. Nancy's letter came at once into Maidlin's mind. " She has some trouble, some burden.
It may be the little sister." Had Nancy been right
in her guess?

Anne did not explain, however. " No, Lindy
has left school. She's just seventeen, and she has
done well; she has the School Certificate, and there
seemed no need for her to stay. She has no wish
to go to college and train for teaching, so it seemed
better she should leave and find some other work."

" I remember she said she needed a job. I
thought it was a joke."

" No, it was in earnest. She'll have to find
something to do."

" And what does she want to do?"

The cloud deepened on Anne's face. " I can't
—I'd like——"

Maidlin spoke hurriedly. " Miss Bellanne, forgive me! I didn't mean to seem inquisitive. You're
still very new friends and you may not care to tell
me. It seems impossible that you've been here only
two days, but it is true, and it's too soon for you to
feel able to tell me things, I know. I ought not to
have asked you."

" Oh, please!" Anne cried. " Please don't feel like that! I'd love to talk to somebody, but—it's hard to know what to do. Lindy's very difficult at times, though you haven't seen anything of it. It's only because she can't have what she wants. She feels thwarted, and she's inclined to believe it's my fault; she doesn't quite understand the difficulties. She'd be all right if she could see any way to start on the career she's craving for. I don't want to gossip about her; but she has a great wish, and I can't help her to her desire, and she's pledged me not to talk of it to anybody, not even you. She's terribly shy about it, and she made me promise."

Maidlin's eyes had filled with eager interest. " I won't ask questions. Perhaps she'll tell me presently. You mean there's something she wants to do and you can't see that it's possible?"

" I can't see how she can get the training she wants. Only the best will satisfy her. It's out of the question; we can't afford it. At the moment I've no job at all; I expect Miss Rowney told you."

" Don't tell me, if you'd rather not!" Maidlin began.

" I don't mind if it's about myself. We had a big house in The Wirral—oh, don't you know The Wirral?" as Maidlin looked at her blankly. " It's a most lovely part of Cheshire, between the rivers, the Mersey and the Dee, with heather-covered commons and red rocks and paths and wild flowers and old villages; how we loved it! Our father was in business in Liverpool, but he failed and the shock killed him. Everything had to be sold, and there wasn't much left for the two of us. Lindy was at a good school and I kept her there, while I went to Manchester and took a thorough training in cookery. A friend who had a cake-shop asked me to join her, and I put the very little money I had into the venture. She let me down badly." Anne's lips pinched. " I'd rather not tell you about that; it was quite a shock. She had misled me about the prospects of the place, and we didn't do well. We struggled on for a time, but she didn't pull her weight and it was too much for me. The shop had to close down, and my money was gone. I collapsed with 'flu, and kind Miss Rowney asked me to The Grange, on the suggestion of a girl who lives in the house where we have rooms."

" I should think your 'flu was chiefly shock," Maidlin said with deep sympathy. " Then you are without a future as well as Belinda?"

" At the moment. But of course I shall find something to do. It won't be difficult; I have good certificates, and cooking is always wanted."

" Yes, that's true." Maidlin looked at her thoughtfully. " You won't start another cake-shop?"

" I don't know," Anne said restlessly. " I haven't made up my mind. Cake-shops are risky; there are so many of them. I could only go as assistant, in any case; I haven't more capital to invest. I can always find good jobs if I'm willing to go as cook in some house, but—there are things to be said for and against that."

Maidlin gave her another quick look of sympathy. " It's rather a different life from being owner of a cake-shop. I do see your dilemma."

"I'm not really snobbish," Anne broke out. "But if I once go into service as one of the maids in a big house, shall I ever be able to get back to my own place?"

"In the other part of the house," Maidlin assented. "But you wouldn't be exactly one of the maids; the cook in a big establishment is a very important person. I should be terrified if I had to interview the cook at Kentisbury Castle! Even Rosamund— my friend, the Countess—pretends to be alarmed if she has to say that anything is wrong. But she does it, because she knows; she's a trained cook herself, just as you are, with the highest possible certificates, and her cook knows it and is very careful what she does. You'd have quite a good position, if you decided to do real cooking. All the same, I see your point; it needs thinking about."

"Lindy doesn't want me to do it," Anne said gravely. "She's convinced that she'll get her training somehow, and that some day she'll be famous, and she doesn't want me to be living in kitchens, even ducal ones."

"Lindy's a very intriguing young person! I won't ask questions," Maidlin said, "but I can see how she feels. It's difficult for you both."

Anne's eyes swept over the green garth and the grey stone walls and the pointed arches of the doorways. "I feel if I can have a little while here, in all these ancient peaceful places, I may perhaps find the way out. At least it will help me to see things more clearly. I'm deeply grateful to you for making it possible. As for Lindy, I believe you could help her, but not until she tells you her ambition. So long as she binds me to silence I can't do anything. But she has no job to go home to, any more than I have. If she'd be the least use to you I wish you'd keep her for a time. She can look for work when she's ready for it; if you are really shorthanded I know she'd be delighted to help. You could trust her with those children. If she was definitely in charge, she'd take great care of them and they'd never know she was doing it."

" It would solve our problem." Maidlin spoke eagerly. " We are short of help at the moment. I expected a friend from Switzerland to stay with us, but her mother has been taken ill, and Cecily can't leave her. Mary not only has her proofs to do, but has been asked for a serial, and it's wanted as soon as possible. She's always prepared to put her work aside, but I feel she ought not to lose chances, and she'd be disappointed if she had to say she couldn't do the serial in time. It means I must take charge of the children all day; I can't be continually dumping them on their aunt and cousins next door."

" And you have your music. That must mean work."

" I have to prepare for this next concert. There are quartettes, as well as solos, and I shall have to go to town to rehearse. And I want to go to Kentisbury quite often; Rosamund has begged me to stay, but I can't do that just now. I shall have to take the twinnies every time I go, unless I can find someone to look after them at home."

" You really seem to need somebody," Anne

agreed. " Would Lindy be enough help to you? Shouldn't they have a governess, or go to school?"

" School is the way out, of course. But Joy—their mother—will be home during the summer, and she may just possibly decide to take them back with her in the autumn. It's been talked of several times. So we're waiting to know her plans. I give the twins lessons, and so does Mary. Their music is good already; we've started them on piano and they have small violins, though Elizabeth insists that she means to be a 'cellist, so that they can play trios with their mother or me! I—or Cecily when she's here—talk French to them, and we do all the usual things in an elementary way. Why shouldn't your Lindy take over their English lessons and sums, leaving the French and music to me? For the rest of the day she could play with them. She's exactly what I want."

" Then do, please, make use of her!" Anne cried. " There's nothing she or I would like more. She was a prefect at school; she must be used to handling juniors."

" Better and better! Suppose you lend her to us for three or four months?"

" I'll be only too delighted!"

" Then let's go and tell her," Maidlin suggested. " Or rather, ask her; we mustn't take her for granted! I'll call the three of them and we'll hear what the twinnies have to say about it."

CHAPTER VIII

MISS BELINDA

" BELINDA BELLANNE! Elizabeth and Margaret!"
The call rang across the cloister garth. Maidlin
could make her voice heard for a considerable distance when she chose.

The twins and Lindy came racing from the refectory stairs.

" They've been showing me the pictures on the
tiles in the floor," Lindy explained.

" What's the matter, Aunty Maid?" Elizabeth
asked.

" Nothing, but we want to speak to you, all three
of you."

" Is it important?" Margaret demanded.

" Perhaps it will be rather important," Maidlin
smiled.

" Then come and say it in the parlour. That's
the proper place!" Margaret shouted, and dashed
ahead of them to the dark little slip of a room, close
to the chapter-house.

" Margaret, don't be absurd!" Maidlin protested.

But Margaret was determined that the news
should be imparted with due ceremony. " This is
the talking-place," and she squatted on the ground.
" Now tell us, Aunty Maid!"

" Sit on that, silly girl." Elizabeth hurled a
cushion at her.

" I aren't! I mean, I'm not." Margaret tucked the cushion beneath her, however. " You can have half, Twin."

Elizabeth crouched on a very small portion, then rose, saying firmly: " I'd rather stand up, thank you. What's the perhaps-rather-important thing, Aunty Maid? Do you know about it, Aunty Nan?"

Anne nodded, watching Belinda.

" Lindy, will you stay with us for a while, perhaps for the summer, and help Mary-Dorothy and me to take care of these bad girls?"

" We aren't that!" Margaret shouted. " We only like adventures! Daddy said we were the adventurous and enterprising daughters!"

" And you've lived up to it," Maidlin agreed.

" Oh, Aunty Belinn, do, do stay with us!" Elizabeth danced in glee. " It would be fun! You could give us our lessons!"

" We'd have lovely adventures," Margaret added.

Lindy's face blazed in delight. " Really and truly—honest? You do think I'd be some use? I'd simply love it; I adore these infants already!"

" Oh, we aren't infants!" The twins spoke together in indignant reproof. " We're nearly nine!"

" Could I be the nursery governess?" Lindy's eyes danced. " I'll be Miss Belinda, and I'll make out a time-table for their lessons. Do let me be Miss Belinda!"

Elizabeth gave a gurgle of amusement. " We'll have to be awful good if you're Miss Belinda."

" Don't want to be good. Twin, you know you don't want to be good always," Margaret urged.

" Perhaps not quite always. But it would be awful fun to do sums with Aunty Belinn."

" Don't be too sure of that!" Lindy's tone was stern. " I can be frightfully strict!"

" Don't you go to school?" Elizabeth seized Lindy's hand and gazed up into her face, in a confiding gesture which was characteristic of her.

" Certainly not! I'm grown up," Lindy said haughtily. " I tell you, I'm Miss Belinda. But I was at school till four days ago," she added with a laugh. " I was a frightfully important Big Girl, and all the little ones thought I was somebody to be frightened of, because I could give them lines and bad marks."

" Will you give us those things?" Elizabeth asked doubtfully.

" We'll try to manage without bad marks," Maidlin said. " If you're good girls, Miss Belinda won't need to punish you."

" Miss Belinda!" Elizabeth chuckled again. " It does sound cross! And she isn't a bit like that, really."

" Wait and see, Miss Marchwood," Lindy retorted.

Elizabeth giggled and skipped about the parlour in delight. " It's going to be fun! I'll like doing sums with you!"

" May I make out a proper time-table, and have exercise books, and do everything like a real school?" Lindy looked at Maidlin eagerly.

" The more like school the better, I should say."
Maidlin smiled at her.

" Just like real school," Elizabeth agreed.

" What happens when we're bad?" Margaret
demanded.

" Something too awful for words," Lindy said
mysteriously. " We won't talk about it. Perhaps
you won't ever be bad."

" Perhaps not," but Margaret sounded not very
hopeful.

" Come and make plans for the real school."
Elizabeth seized Lindy's hand, looking up at her
appealingly.

" In here. This is the talking-place," Margaret
said instantly. " You other people go away. Now,
Miss Belinda, you sit on a cushion and tell us what
we're going to do."

Anne and Maidlin obediently removed themselves and strolled about the garth, with occasional
glances into the dark little parlour, where, at the
sunlit entrance, three heads were close together,
one fair, two dark red.

" This is going to be a success," Maidlin smiled
at Anne. " I do feel so thankful!"

" It's nothing to what I feel," Anne assured her.
" To have Lindy happily occupied means everything to me. She's never troublesome when she's
interested and busy."

" I shall give her a small salary—oh yes! You
must allow that. She's going to be very useful to
us, and she'll feel so much more important," Maidlin said earnestly. " And we shall be taking her

time, when she might be preparing for some other job."

"It's far too good of you!" Anne protested. "Just to live here, in this beautiful place, would be enough payment for Lindy. It will be a glorious holiday for her. She has missed her home, and our old garden, and the commons she loved so much, and the sea, more than she knows. She hates city life."

"We can't give her the sea, but the country here is lovely. I hope you'll stay for some time, too, Miss Bellanne. You need a real holiday after the rough time you've had, and you can see for yourself that we have plenty of room. You won't be in the way; it will be jolly to have you, if you won't mind Mary and me being a bit wrapped up in our own concerns at times. We're both rather like that, I'm afraid," Maidlin confessed, a smile in the depths of her dark eyes. "Mary-Dorothy gets lost in her latest story, and I go off into dreams of music. We try to do our duty to the outside world, but we each keep an inside life and we're apt to retire into it and neglect other people."

"I haven't seen much sign of it so far," Anne remarked. "Perhaps Miss Devine was dreaming when Margaret ran away and climbed the tree, but you seem to think of everything and to manage things perfectly."

"Mary was telling Elizabeth a story and she didn't notice that Margaret had slipped away. The children keep us both awake, of course; you have to be very much on the spot when they're about.

There's no dreaming for any one who's in charge of Elizabeth!"

" I thought Margaret was the difficult one!" Anne exclaimed.

" You don't know them yet. Elizabeth has the ideas; she had said to Margaret, ' We'd better climb a tree to show Andy we really can do it,' and Margaret seized her chance. Elizabeth owned up to me at night, and Margaret told Mary she was sorry she'd run away. They're dears, but their father was an adventurer—an explorer and big-game hunter in Central Africa, Andrew March-wood—and they have some of his nature. Their mother used to explore in a small way too; she says she was always a wandering gipsy, as a girl. Ivor Quellyn told her the twins were her adventurous and enterprising daughters; that's what Margaret quoted just now. He was right; they certainly are. But Lindy knows how to handle them, I believe. You will stay with us, both for her sake and ours, won't you?"

" You're more than kind. It means as much to me as to Lindy to be in a beautiful place. But couldn't you drop ' Miss Bellanne ' and call me Nan?"

" It would sound more friendly," Maidlin assented. " I'd like to. It's a dear little name."

" And I shall say ' Miss Maid,' as everybody does. It suits you."

" Oh, must you stick to ' Miss '?" That smile glimmered in Maidlin's eyes again.

" I like it. You are ' Miss Maid,' " Anne said firmly.

" We'll take the children back to the house; it's bedtime. And I must practise. I've done nothing to-day yet, because you were in bed." Maidlin called the twins to come.

" We're making plans," Elizabeth said with dignity. " Tell you later, Aunty Maid."

" Miss Belinda has marvellous ideas," Margaret cried, dancing on ahead.

When they had gone upstairs with Nelly, their nurse, Maidlin went to the piano. " You two can go and rest, or stay here, just as you please," she said. " But I must work in earnest for an hour."

Lindy dropped into a big chair from which she could watch as well as listen. Anne, sitting near the window, found her eyes wandering round the beautiful lounge hall, with its old furniture, family portraits, and stained-glass windows; then she looked out at the lawn with its gathering shadows under the trees and pale daffodils and narcissus; and then at the slight figure of the girl at the piano as her rich voice filled the house.

The twins, on their way to bed, hung over the railing of the gallery to listen, until drawn away by Nelly. Lindy sat with rapt eyes fixed on Maidlin's face. This was no longer " Miss Maid," but Madalena di Ravarati of the Free Trade Hall.

Maidlin seemed absorbed in her practising, but she was aware of Lindy's enjoyment, and the thought flashed through her mind: " Is it music the child wants to do? I wonder how soon she'll tell me. Pity she's so shy about it; perhaps I could help her, if it's anything to do with music. But I must wait; it must come from herself. I've fixed her here for some time to come. Surely she'll trust me soon."

" Oh, please! What's that lovely thing?" Lindy begged, as Maidlin paused to study her music intently.

Maidlin smiled across at her. " A song from *In a Persian Garden*. Dr. Robertson's going to send me the whole cycle of songs; he's suggested I should sing it for him in June. He says he must keep me human; I mustn't sing only Angel music. Here's another little bit!"

Lindy crept into Anne's room late that night. " Nan, you aren't asleep? Oh, Nan, isn't it marvellous? Aren't they kind? This new idea of Miss Maid's—I want to cry, I'm so keen."

" I knew you were pleased. You'll make good, Lin. You'll be very careful of those twins, won't you?"

" Pleased! I couldn't say much. I nearly wept as it was. I could have danced and sung and shouted all at once."

" Be careful what you teach them and what you say before them. Don't let them pick up too much school slang," Anne advised.

" They'll pick up anything they can," Lindy grinned. " They're as sharp as needles, and like magpies for catching on to things. They'll be easy to teach, but not so easy to manage; I've been watching them while they talked. So long as it's all a game they'll learn anything; but if they're bored it will be different. I don't think I could make them do anything they'd decided not to do."

" No, you'll have to lead, not drive, them."

" Am I good enough, Nan? I thought I was ready to be grown up, but to-night I feel I've been rushed into it and I'm really only a kid still. I'm not good enough, am I?"

" Miss Maid thinks you are. That's all that matters."

" Wasn't that music heavenly? And we'll hear it every day. You didn't tell her, Nan? No, I know you didn't. Please don't say anything! I want to be Miss Belinda, the nursery governess!"

" My advice is, trust Miss Maid and tell her everything," Anne said. " Now go to bed, Lindy! I won't ask to hear your plans. We'll see the results soon, I expect."

CHAPTER IX

AN EMPTY SCHOOLROOM

" MISS MAID, you know that funny little room opening off the cloisters?" Lindy asked during breakfast, which, to her delight and Anne's, was spread on a table carried out on to the terrace in the sunshine. " The twins say their mother used to sleep there."

Maidlin raised her eyebrows. " Joy's bedroom? It was once part of the house of the lay-brothers, who weren't proper monks. When Joy's aunt was the caretaker of the Abbey—I told you that story— Joy slept in that little room. What about it?"

" May we have it for a schoolroom, please?"

Maidlin put down her cup and stared at her.

"A schoolroom? But why? Is it big enough?"

"Wouldn't it be too dark?" Anne asked, puzzled.

"It isn't really dark. We could go out to the garth for some lessons, and if visitors came to see the Abbey we'd go inside again. We'd only need three chairs and a table—I suppose we can't have desks—and our own lesson-books on the shelves," Lindy pleaded.

"But what's the idea? Wouldn't you be much more comfortable in the nursery?" Maidlin queried. "It's big and light and sunny, and the twins have all their possessions there."

"Yes, much! But it *is* the nursery!" Lindy spoke with intense eagerness. "I want them to feel they're going to school every day, at a regular time, and so the school must be somewhere outside the house. They'll be much more keen; it will feel more like the real thing. If we just do lessons in the nursery they'll be inclined to play about, and Nelly will be there, and I shan't be able to keep them at it. But if we go to school—go right *out* to go to school—they'll settle down to work and it will feel more real. I'm thinking of the psychological effect," she ended gravely, but with dancing eyes.

"May we laugh?" Maidlin pleaded, her eyes laughing already, as Anne gave a shout and Mary Devine joined in. "I don't want to hurt your feelings. You're perfectly right, Miss Belinda."

"Laugh as much as you like, so long as you let me have my schoolroom," Lindy said cheerfully. "You do think it's sensible, don't you?"

"Absolutely. Until the novelty wears off the

twinnies will love starting out for school every morning," Maidlin assured her.

" If they get tired of it we can come back here. It would be much nicer," Lindy acknowledged. " That nursery, with a big table by the window, would be a marvellous place to work. But I want things to seem different."

" It's a brilliant idea. We'll furnish your school-room to-day. That little room!" Maidlin said. " It has its history, like the rest of the Abbey. First the lay-brothers; then Joy slept there. When the Abbey was given to Joan and this house became Joy's, Joan kept that room for her own use, and she slept there when the school was invited to come here and this house was crowded out. Ros and I slept there on the night the twins were born, when Joy nearly died and we were turned out of this place; they wanted us to go to the Manor, but we begged to be allowed to stay in the Abbey. Actually we slept on the cloister steps and Ros took care of me like a mother; then when it was all safely over I went to bed in the small room and slept for hours. Betty, who lives in the village, was carried in there after her accident. You slept there the first time you came to the Hall, Mary, because the house was full of May-day visitors. And years afterwards, when I brought Biddy and her baby home from France, they had that little room. And now it's to be the schoolroom for the twins and Miss Belinda!"

The twins joined in the furnishing of their new study with enthusiasm. Mary Devine found a big map of Europe, taken from an old *Geographic Magazine*; this was pinned on the wall, and the children looked serious and eyed " Miss Belinda " with new respect. Maidlin delved into her treasures and produced a large chart of musical notes which Joy had made for her years before, and this was hung opposite the map. The twins knew their notes well enough, but this was new, and they shouted with joy over Great-Grandfather Breve and Grandfather Semi-Breve, who had large round white faces and straggly hair and beards, and Mr. and Mrs. Minim, who had one long leg each, and their four black sons and daughters, young Misses and Master Crotchet, and the Quaver family of dancing black children, and the Semi-Quaver babies. Even Margaret could never forget how many Crotchet and Quaver descendants belonged to the family of Breve, with those lively figures always before her eyes.

Lindy begged for a supply of pencils, black and coloured, and of various exercise-books, so that each subject could have its separate note-book, and Maidlin asked Mary to make out a list and write to Wycombe for supplies.

" The only thing we need now is a jar for flowers on that shelf," Lindy announced. " We must do botany, so we ought to have a vase for our specimens. We're going to grow things in water—acorns and bulbs; we'll have a forest of tiny trees, and then we'll plant them out in a corner somewhere. My school children want to watch the roots come out at the bottom."

" You really have some bright ideas, Miss Belinda!" Maidlin exclaimed.

Lindy's plans did not all go smoothly, however.

For two days she and the twins set off punctually at twenty-five minutes past nine, the children greatly amused at being led away promptly at the exact minute and feeling very important as school-girls, carrying attaché-cases with books and pencil-boxes, and slices of cake for " elevenses." They worked steadily and enjoyed every moment, and would have gone back to school in the afternoon, if their governess had not insisted with great firmness on a walk in the woods or a climb on the hills, during which she unobtrusively watched them all the time.

Just after tea, on the second day of school, Maidlin was at the piano and the twins were trans-lating her snatches of tunes into movement—danc-ing, or creeping, or lying down to sleep, as the music suggested—when there came the sound of a motor-horn, and a car drew up below the terrace.

" It's young Mr. Robertson, who was here on Saturday," said Anne from the window.

" Perhaps he's bringing the music his uncle pro-mised me. Why didn't they send it?" Maidlin began.

Anne thought she could guess. " He may be bringing music; I don't know. But he's lifting a gorgeous bunch of roses out of the car," she said.

" Gracious!" Maidlin looked at her with startled eyes. " What is he doing that for?"

" To give them to Miss Belinda, because she was hurt and he helped to carry her home, I expect," Elizabeth suggested.

" No, for me, because I was stuck in the beashly tree!"

" Much more likely to be for Aunty Maid, because you gave her a horrid fright and he wants her to forget about it," Lindy said severely.

Donald, on the terrace, presented the roses to Maidlin, hoping she was not the worse for Saturday's shock and that all the invalids had recovered. " You told me your roses weren't ready yet, so I brought along a few, as a foretaste of summer, with the music from Uncle Jock," he explained.

" These are lovely! We shan't have roses for two months yet. It's really kind of you," Maidlin said. " Everybody's very much all right. Come in and look at them."

" Oh, don't they make a lovely couple?" Lindy murmured. " He's so fair and tall, and she's so dark and neat! Oh, Nan, do you think——?"

" No, I don't," Anne said firmly.

" Oh, why? It would be so jolly for them both!"

Anne shook her head. " We'll have to introduce you. You were only the patient when he saw you before."

Lindy's laugh rang out. " I'm the body!" she announced, as Donald followed Maidlin indoors. " I'm the thing that was on the stretcher."

" You look very much better than you did as a body," he assured her. " There wasn't much wrong with you, evidently."

" I'm the new nursery governess," Lindy informed him. " I'm Miss Belinda Bellanne, and these two are my school."

" Dear me! That's a pity!" he mocked. " You won't be pleased with me, I'm afraid. I've come to propose a picnic for to-morrow." He turned to Maidlin. "Couldn't I come early and run you all down to the seaside for the day? We'd be there in a couple of hours. These two would like to see the sea, I'm sure."

"The seaside!" Margaret gave a shriek of ecstasy. "Oh, you dear darling man! Oh, let's go now!"

"Haven't been to the sea for hundreds of years." Elizabeth danced with joy. "Oh, Aunty Maid, say yes! Could we paddle?"

"No, certainly not! It's early April," Maidlin said ruthlessly. "I don't know; it's very kind, but——"

"Oh, let them come!" he begged. "And you too, of course. I want everybody to come; the old bus will hold quite a crowd. Let's have a jolly day and forget all about being kittens in trees!"

"But what about school?" Lindy protested. "They've just begun. They ought to do their work! Couldn't we go in the afternoon?"

"Too far. We must have the whole day. Oh, give them a holiday! It can't matter much with such babes."

"We aren't babies," Elizabeth said haughtily. "We go to school. We're big now."

"But we like the seaside!" Margaret urged.

Maidlin looked at Lindy. "It's not fair to you, I know. But they don't often go to the sea, and they would enjoy it."

"Lindy likes the sea too," Anne remarked. "She's only being the stern governess."

"Oh, let's go, Aunty Lin! You can be Miss

Belinda the next day," Margaret pleaded. "I'm going! I know I'm going!"

"Would there be any of those machine-things where you put in a penny to make them work?" Elizabeth seized Donald's hand and gazed up into his face in the way which, as she was quite aware, very few people could resist.

"Automatics. I expect so." He laughed down into the eager brown eyes. "We'll look for them, and Miss Belinda shall take you round with a bag of pennies. I expect we'll find some machines on the pier."

"Will there be a pier? Oh, goody!" Margaret began to rush wildly round the hall in excitement. "Did you say to-morrow? What's your name? Uncle what?"

"Uncle Don. I'm promoted." He smiled at Maidlin, a hint of hidden meaning in his eyes.

"Oh no! That doesn't mean you're adopted as one of the family." Maidlin was serenely unconscious of his underlying thought. "These twinnies live in a world of aunts and uncles; they don't believe in ' Miss ' and ' Mr.' Is that the new music? Will you thank Dr. Robertson very warmly for me? I've been longing for it. Please thank him for the roses too, if he sent them as well. We shall all enjoy them."

"The roses are from me," Donald said promptly. "The music is from Doc-Jock."

Maidlin stared at him. "What did you say?"

Donald's laugh rang out. "That's what the orchestra call him; haven't you heard them?"

"I have not! Why do they do it?"

" They may have heard me call him Uncle Jock.
But they've turned it into Doc-Jock. They say
he's too young to be Uncle Jock to them; lots of
them are quite old stagers."

" It might be a friendly title, as it is with the
twins," Maidlin smiled. " He's hardly old enough
to be Uncle to those nice elderly 'cellos and double
basses. Doc-Jock! What a nickname!"

" They always say it. ' Steady, chaps! Here
comes Doc-Jock!' I've heard that often. To-
morrow, then? I'll be here by ten. Thank you so
much for saying yes, Miss Maid."

" Thank *you* for the picnic, Uncle Don!" the
twins shouted after him, as he went back to his car.

" Doc-Jock!" Maidlin said, a smile in her eyes,
as she arranged the roses in a silver bowl on the oak
table in the hall. " It's too bad! But it sounds
friendly. I wonder what he'd say if I called him
Doc-Jock?"

" Try it and see," Anne suggested, looking at
her curiously.

" No, I don't think so; I wouldn't dare. One
doesn't play about with—Doc-Jock! Aren't these
lovely, Nan? It was kind of Donald, wasn't it?"

" Very!" Anne agreed. " He's a nice boy."

" Oh yes! A very jolly boy. I like him very
much."

" Poor Donald!" Anne said to herself, her eyes
on the girl bending over the roses. " I wouldn't give
a threepenny bit for his chances."

CHAPTER X

MRS. SPINDLE BRINGS TROUBLE

THE picnic to the sea was followed two days later by an invitation to a trip to Whipsnade, not very far away across the hills. The radiant delight of the twins was too much for Maidlin; and Anne, and even Miss Belinda, agreed that it would be good for their education to see the Zoo.

On the way home Donald revealed that he had heard of a queer little museum in a Sussex village, where stuffed kittens and rats and guinea-pigs were formed into tableaux of " Cock Robin " and other set pieces, and where there were automatic machines to be set in movement by the insertion of a penny, to Elizabeth's great joy. Nothing would keep the twins from a visit to Bramber, and Maidlin smiled an apology at Miss Belinda for the ruined term.

" Your schoolroom is empty too often. But they'll enjoy it so much, Lindy, and you'll like it too. We'll settle down to work soon. After all, it's still the school holidays, isn't it?"

Mary Devine stayed at home on these picnic days and gratefully seized the chance to go ahead with her work, but Anne was careful always to be in the party, and her eyes were often on Donald and Maidlin in quiet scrutiny.

After the visit to the animal museum she sought Mary during the evening. The twins were in bed;

Lindy had begged for the key and had gone to wander alone in the Abbey; Maidlin was in town, rehearsing her quartettes for *Elijah,* but would be home by ten o'clock.

" Could you spare a few minutes, Mary-Dorothy?" Anne had adopted the family custom of giving Mary her whole name. " Will it interrupt the serial too badly? Or don't you work at night?"

" Not much, if I want to sleep. The serial's going nicely." Mary smiled. " It's always a thrill trying to end the instalments at the right place—to get good ' curtains,' you know. Come in here; you haven't seen my room yet."

" Oh, how pretty!" Anne looked round the brown and gold study, with its ornaments of hand-thrown pottery in the same rich colours, dark chestnut brown and soft old gold. " Is this where you work? No wonder your books are good!"

" Joy arranged it for me." Mary swept the long galley-strips of her proofs aside. " What's the trouble, Nan?"

" Miss Maid and young Donald." Anne dropped on a stool beside the gas-fire and looked up at her.

" I was afraid of it." Mary sank into her big chair. " Are you sure? But nothing has happened? I should know at once. Maid was as calm and happy as usual."

" No, but it will. He expected me to clear out and leave them alone together, in the old castle this afternoon. I didn't take the hint."

" Maid doesn't know, does she?"

" She's quite unconscious. She ought to see

what's coming," Anne exclaimed. " It's obvious to every one else."

" But not to Maid. It wouldn't occur to her. She's such a mixture; very childish in some ways and oddly mature in others. She'll never think of it."

" Then she must be warned," Anne urged. " Or she'll have a shock. Suppose it dawns on her just before this big concert? She's so sensitive; she may take it badly."

" She will," Mary said gravely. " She'll be frightfully upset; she feels things very deeply. Maid has depths which aren't often stirred, but when they are she loses control. She has an Italian temperament hidden under her quiet surface, and it sweeps her off her feet when it's roused."

" I've suspected that, from the depth of feeling in her singing. When she pours out ' O Rest in the Lord ' I feel as if she's pleading with me, and every one, to escape into that rest."

Mary stared at the fire. " I'm afraid," she said simply.

" Somebody ought to wake her up to what young Donald is after!" Anne pleaded. " You know her so much better than I do. She won't marry him, will she?"

" Oh no! He's far too young and unformed. Maid doesn't want to marry, but if she does it will be an older man, a matured personality, someone she can look up to and rely on."

" I've felt that," Anne agreed. " Donald's uncle, Dr. Jock, would suit her!" And she looked at Mary expectantly.

"That verges on gossip." Mary sat up. "We mustn't do that, Anne Bellanne. She'd never forgive me if I talked about her. For you to come to me because you're in trouble about her is all right, but we won't drift into gossip. Oh, how I wish Joy was here!"

There was such distress in her tone that Anne knew she, too, suspected that Maidlin's true romance might be hovering over her. It was hard enough for Maidlin to have to cope with an unwanted suitor, without her beloved guardian to comfort her; but if she were to fall in love, with all the force of her stormy nature, which Anne had dimly sensed, there might be troubled times ahead, for Mary as well as for Maid herself.

"Could any one else speak to her?" Anne ventured. "Lady Jen, at the Manor? She's very fond of her. Or her chum, the Countess?"

Mary, chin in hand, gazed at the fire. "If they discover it for themselves, either of them would do it better than I could. But I couldn't—no, I couldn't tell them; that again would seem to Maid like gossip about her. Perhaps Rosamund or Jen will guess. That would be best. Don't give Donald a chance to see her alone, for a few days, Nan; we'll try to have *Elijah* safely over before the explosion comes. I'm glad she didn't let them send their car to fetch her to-night; Donald might have driven her home. It's better Frost should go for her."

"Donald wanted to do it, but she laughed at him. It would have been silly; he would have been very late in getting back to town."

" Maid always prefers to have Frost, after she's been singing. The music works her up, and, as she says, Frost doesn't talk," Mary said. " She has a quiet hour alone in the car to calm down; the last thing she wants is to be brought home by chattering friends. I'm afraid we gave you a very poor dinner to-night, but Cook seemed so poorly that I sent her off to bed early and the meal suffered. I was glad Maid was dining in town."

" What's the matter with Cook?" Anne asked idly. " She seems a nice young woman. Lindy's fascinated by her name—Mrs. Spindle!"

Mary laughed. " Spindle is an old name hereabouts, but you've had to avoid the village, because of the measles. Susan—yes, she's Susan Spindle—came here to work when she left school, at fourteen; she was keen on cooking, so Joy let her learn from the cook of those days, and then, as Cook spoke well of her, sent her away to have training and to get experience. She came back, but married a cousin in the village, so her name is still Spindle; she was unfortunate, for he died two years ago, leaving her with a baby. The child is with the grandmother, and Susan came back here as Cook. She does very well on the whole."

" What's wrong with her to-night?"

" A sudden heavy cold and very bad headache. I saw her, and her eyes were just streaming, and I think she was feverish. I sent her off to bed at once."

Anne turned a startled face to her. " But that sounds like measles! Has she been to the village lately?"

Mary grew white. " I never thought of that. Oh, *no*! Oh, Nan, not measles—in the house! With Joy away!"

" It would be a blow, of course, but measles isn't so deadly," Anne said stoutly. " The children might not take it. They aren't often with Cook; perhaps they haven't been near her for a day or two. I'll ask Lindy, shall I?"

" They've been so carefully guarded. They've never had anything," Mary said unsteadily.

" They'll need to begin some time. They won't get through life without having the usual things. But it will be a pity if it happens while their mother is away," Anne conceded.

" A pity!" Mary rose with a groan. " I'll find out if Cook has been to the village. We gave strict orders that no one must go till the quarantine was over."

" I'll find out from Lindy if the children have been near Mrs. Spindle," Anne said. " I'll come back and tell you."

They met again in a few minutes. There was tragedy in Anne's face and despair in Mary's.

" Lindy and the twins were in the kitchen just before the children went to bed," Anne said. " They were playing with the new kitten. Lindy noticed Cook's cold, so she took the kitten's basket out into the yard; it was thoughtful of her, but the mischief may have been done. She couldn't know what was the matter."

" Susan went down to the village to see her boy a fortnight ago, just after the first case of measles was discovered," Mary said grimly. " I've rung up the doctor. If he confirms our fears, I shall send her off to hospital, if possible before Maid comes home."

" Oh, good!" Anne cried. " You have grappled with the situation! I was afraid——" She checked herself.

" That I'd go to pieces and do nothing. I had a shock; I was utterly taken aback. But there's nothing else to do. We can't keep a case of measles in the house. Now, Nan, there's one thing more. Maid mustn't know to-night. We'll tell her in the morning."

Anne agreed. " It would be cruel to meet her with news of trouble late at night. But can you keep it from her?"

" There's a letter from Joy. That will take up her thoughts. If we don't tell her she won't notice anything."

" I won't say a word. Will the doctor come in time?"

" He's coming at once. He'll be keen to get Susan away; he feels as we do about the children in Joy's absence."

The ambulance carrying Susan Spindle to the hospital had been gone for half an hour before Maidlin arrived, radiantly happy after her rehearsal.

" It's such joy to sing with those lovely voices! We had a marvellous time," she said. " The music's wonderful, and Doc-Jock seemed pleased. We're all looking forward to the concert now. And he does want me for the *Persian Garden*, as I'd hoped. I'll love to sing in it. He wants a group of solos as well; it's at Queen's Hall, in June."

" Oh, congrats, Maid! I know you hoped he'd use you," Mary said. " Look, Madalena! Here's a treat for you!"

" Joy's letter! I was hoping for it," and Maidlin settled down to read the letter, while Mary brought milk and sandwiches.

Anne slipped away, after a few moments, and went up to bed.

" All right?" Lindy crept to her door.

" She never asked a single question; too busy with her letter and her music." Anne told of the invitation for the new concert. " I know now what you do all alone in the Abbey, Lin!"

" Yes—sing. I have to let out sometimes, and no one will hear me there. The caretaker's promised not to give me away; she seems to like my squalling. I wander round and moan out all the things I know, and if I really want to let myself go I plunge into the parlour or some other little dark place where nobody could possibly hear me."

" You're an ass to be so shy," Anne said. " But as you've kept it to yourself for so long you'd better keep quiet for a while longer. Miss Maid won't have time to think about your career at present."

" My hat, no! Not if the twins go down with measles. I say, Nan, I believe I can really help her. Shall I tell you how?"

" You? I believe I can," Anne retorted. " Yes, tell me, if there's anything you think you can do. I'm going to offer to take on the kitchen work for them."

" Oh, cheers! You sport! Well, now, listen about me," and Lindy curled up on the bed and spoke earnestly.

CHAPTER XI

BELLANNES TO THE RESCUE

" OH—MARY!" Maidlin wailed. " Oh, say it's all a mistake! We've tried to be so careful! Oh, it is hard lines!"

" I know." Mary spoke almost bitterly. " I'm not usually bloodthirsty, but I would like to do something really fierce to Susan. It's so unnecessary; surely she could have waited!"

She had carried in a tray to Maidlin's room and had broken the news while they shared their early tea.

" I could wring Susan Spindle's neck," Maidlin said savagely. " I'm glad you sent her off. Joy will never let her come back. Mary, you've had a bad night," and her eyes searched Mary's face keenly. " It was kind of you not to tell me when I came home, but it's been bothering you. Couldn't you sleep?"

" Not much," Mary confessed. " I didn't like to feel I was hiding something from you. I kept wondering how I'd tell you."

" I'm sorry. You should have told me and let me share the trouble," Maidlin said remorsefully.

There was a tap on the door and a voice asked:
" May we come in? We know you're discussing

things and we want to help. We both have useful
suggestions to make. Don't keep us outside!"

" Of the mess we're in, or of my room?" Maidlin called in reply. " Please come in; but don't
make personal remarks. I'm only half awake and
not fit to be seen."

She lay on her pillows and looked at them, her
hair hanging in two thick plaits over her pink dressing-gown. " You're all up very early! You make
me feel thoroughly lazy. But you weren't in town
till late at night. Well, Anne Bellanne, what do
you think of the situation?"

" That I'd like to lynch Mrs. Spindle. But Mary-
Dorothy has dealt with her, and I do admire the
promptness with which she acted," Anne began.

Maidlin's eyes smiled at Mary. " I'm very grateful to her. Susan had to go, but I'm glad I didn't
have to decide to send her. Mary's been a brick
as usual."

" The doctor would have decided, if I hadn't.
Have you two had your tea?" Mary looked at
Anne and Lindy. " Breakfast may be a little late;
I'm going down to see to it. The other maids aren't
much use at cooking. Now what about these sug-
gestions?"

A thought flashed into Maidlin's mind, and she
looked quickly at Anne Bellanne. But no; one
could not ask a guest to become the cook, even
though cooking happened to be her job. She sighed.
It would be a nuisance finding a new cook and
having a stranger in the house, but Mary must not
be allowed to do it.

" I'm doing the breakfast," Anne said firmly.

" And the lunch, and the tea, and the dinner. If you'll trust me, that is. Won't you hand over Mrs. Spindle's job to me? Permanently, if you like; I'd be glad to cook for you; but certainly for the time."

" Oh, Nan! Would you?" Maidlin cried. " It would make things so much easier! But we mustn't allow it; it's your holiday!"

" I've had a lovely week, and I'm as fit as I ever shall be, while I've no work to do. That's settled, then. I am now Mrs. Spindle."

" Oh no! You're Mistress Bellanne." Maidlin's sigh of relief was almost a sob. " Oh, Nan, you are kind! That will be a great help!"

Mary's face had lit up. " I call that a really generous offer! How glad we shall be! Oh, I hope you'll stay—Mistress Bellanne!"

Anne laughed. " I like my title! Cooks are always called ' Mrs.,' aren't they? Now let Miss Belinda speak!"

" What does Lindy want to suggest? If she has an idea that is even half as practical as yours, I shall leap out of bed and embrace her," Maidlin said.

" Nan says you'll fall on my neck," Lindy agreed. " Miss Maid, the kiddies may not take the measles, after all, but if they do I want you to keep away from them—you'd have to, anyway, because of your concerts—and let me be shut up with them. I'll play with them and tell them stories while they're ill, and then we'll go on playing at lessons when they're getting over it."

" Oh, we couldn't do that!" Maidlin and Mary

spoke together. " You'd catch the thing from them!"

" No, that's the point," Lindy said eagerly. " Measles doesn't like me. We had it at school last year, and the girls who sat on each side of me had it and most of those in my dorm., and I was with them and I never took it. The doctor kept watching me, and at last he laughed and said I must be a measles immune—a person who didn't have measles. So it will be perfectly safe for me to be with the twins. I'll keep them amused for you."

Maidlin looked doubtfully at Anne. " What do you think? It would be an enormous help, but ought we to risk it?"

" We could ask the doctor," Mary began.

" I had measles when I was twelve, and Lindy was only four," Anne said. " We were together, but she never took it. It seems to me she's the right one to nurse the twins, if nursing should be needed."

" If nursing is needed we shall have a real nurse," Maidlin said firmly. " We're taking no risks with the twins. We'll have someone who knows what to do, whatever happens; we don't want complications, and we haven't had experience. But Lindy would be simply invaluable as an assistant, to keep the children happy and amused, if she's really willing to be in quarantine with them."

" I'll go into the garden for exercise, or into the Abbey after it's closed to the public." Lindy grinned at thought of her private concerts in the Abbey. " Cheerio! That's settled. Don't worry about it any more. If the kids do go measly we'll all pull them through together."

" They won't have it badly. They're so splendidly well," Anne said.

" You are comforting, you two!" Maidlin sighed. " You're so matter-of-fact and sensible about it. You can't realise that the twins have been brought up as if they were royalty and kept away from any possible infection, because for seven years they were all Joy had to live for. So you just don't know what a tragedy it is to Mary and me that they may perhaps be ill while Joy's so far away. And so you can be calm about it, and say—' Oh, they won't have it badly!' It's really very helpful."

" It sounds callous, I'm afraid," Anne said.

" No, just reasonable; we're unreasonable about it. It's silly to be so much upset because the children have been in contact with measles; as Miss Belinda says, they may not have taken it, after all. But we know what it will mean to Joy, and you haven't even met her. Shall I tell her when I write?"

" Don't say anything until we're sure," Mary suggested.

" But if it happens we'd have to cable and she'd have had no warning. It would be cruel. A letter takes some days to go," Maidlin said thoughtfully. " If I could plan it so that she'd hear of the danger about the time the twins were due to start, then she wouldn't have a long while of anxiety, and we could cable ' Safe ' or ' Ill,' and she'd have been prepared."

" That's much better than my way," Mary agreed. " Can you time your letter?"

" I'll try. Joy ought to be prepared. Now how are we going to manage? We mustn't say a word to the twins themselves, but they'll have to be kept away from everybody. They'll want to know why they mustn't go to the Manor as usual."

" Lady Jen won't want them near her little family," Anne remarked.

" Both the Manor and Kentisbury must be out of bounds," Mary said. " It won't be easy to explain to the children."

" They'll feel they are being isolated." Maidlin pondered the situation. " Could we explain to Donald Robertson and ask his help? If he took them for several picnics they might not realise that they hadn't been to the Manor for some days."

Anne looked at Mary, but Mary avoided her eyes. " We'll think it over, Maid. ' Uncle Don ' might not want to take measles contacts about the country. I think we should tell him what has happened, and then keep the twins at home and let Miss Belinda go on with their education. Her schoolroom has been empty a good deal lately. We must chance their questions; perhaps Jen will take her five to The Grange to see the new paint and papers. Didn't Nancy say the work was nearly finished?"

Maidlin assented. " I'll ring Jen up as soon as I've dressed. I'm very much obliged to you, Nan and Lindy—or I should say, Mistress Bellanne and Miss Belinda! But if you wouldn't mind going out of my room now, I'd like to get up."

" Must you put your hair up?" Lindy insinu-

ated. " It's glorious hanging down; just marvellous! Couldn't you wear it like that for the Albert
Hall?"

" I said no personal remarks," Maidlin said
severely. " Go away, Lindy Bellanne!"

" I go to take possession of the kitchen, and of
Mrs. Spindle's overalls!" Anne proclaimed.

" Bellannes to the rescue!" Lindy shouted.

CHAPTER XII

DONALD'S LETTER

JEN, at the Manor, was as matter-of-fact about
possible measles as the Bellanne girls had been. She
agreed to take her little family, and her four-
months-old baby, to The Grange to inspect the new
paint and papers, and so forestall any questions on
the part of the twins. She pointed out, however,
that as the infection could have come only through
Mrs. Spindle there was no hurry; the twins, even if
infected, could not pass on the trouble yet; for a
week, at least, they could be considered safe.

" As for Susie Spindle," she said, " I'm sorry
you've had to fling her out, but you had no choice.
She had measles at the Hall fifteen years ago, when
Joan and Joy had it, though she didn't take it
from them; it was in the village, and her home was
there. If the twinnies develop it, take care they
don't get chills on top of the measles, Maid. Joy
nearly died; oh, didn't you know? It was long
before your time, of course. But she didn't nearly

die of measles; it was pneumonia, because she would talk to me at an open window while she was still feverish. She was an idiot, and we told her so. Don't let Margaret hang out of open windows! Lindy Bellanne will take care she doesn't; you're lucky to have her.''

'' We're lucky to have Anne too. To find a new cook right on the spot is marvellous.'' Maidlin rang off and went to talk to Mary.

'' I must tell the Robertsons. As *Elijah* is next week, it will be over before the children could show any signs of illness. But after that, Doctor Jock mustn't expect anything from me for a few weeks; I couldn't go to town, or sing in public, if the twins were ill. I shall tell Donald that we'll have no more picnics at present; it's time Lindy's schoolroom was used in earnest.''

Mary and Anne, for their own reasons, agreed with this programme, and hoped Donald would take the hint and leave them in peace. That was too much to expect, however, and he arrived promptly, laden with roses once more, to beg for a few days' grace before lessons began.

'' I'd planned to take the infants to Kew Gardens. They'd be intrigued by the pagoda and the orchid-house and the pitcher-plants. And I want to have one really long day and run you all across to Cheddar to see the caves. It isn't so very far; you're nearly at Oxford already. Won't you relent and let us have those two outings at least, Miss Maid?''

Maidlin looked at him gravely. A question had begun to torment her vaguely, though she had not faced it yet. Why was it only Donald who came? He was always alone, on the plea that his mother and uncle had work and engagements and that the car would be uncomfortably crowded with any more grown-ups.

She looked at Mary Devine. " Shall we, Mary? Would you care to come? I've always wanted to see Cheddar."

" I love Kew. We used to go when I lived in town," Mary confessed. " Would you have me? We couldn't tear Nan from her kitchen; she's re-organising everything and is extremely happy."

" She's terribly thrilled." Maidlin smiled up at Donald. " She's taken over the cooking, and she's replanning shelves and cupboards and having a marvellous time. She won't go to Kew and Cheddar, but I think perhaps Mary will. Her work has been behaving nicely lately."

" It will go still better if I leave it for a day or two. I always feel a little stale after reading proofs."

" Oh, do come along with us!" Donald said, as heartily as he could, bravely hiding all sign of disappointment. " We'll freshen you up and banish the staleness."

So Mary took Anne's place in the car, and the twins and Lindy had two more days of rapturous enjoyment.

" Safely over!" Mary whispered to Anne, while Maidlin was practising. " But you're right. He wanted to get her alone. I was very much in the way."

" Shall you speak to her? You can say you've

seen it for yourself now. No need to tell her I'd noticed anything."

"That's true. But I'd rather wait till after the concert."

So, it seemed, would Donald. He accepted the edict that lessons must now begin in earnest and did not appear for several days, and Mary thankfully awaited events and said nothing.

The day before the great occasion Maidlin drove to town for a final rehearsal, and on her return slipped an envelope into Lindy's hand with a smile.

"Stalls for to-morrow night, Miss Belinda. You and Nan will come, won't you? I think you said you liked going to concerts?"

"Oh, Miss Maid!" Lindy sprang up with a shout. "Are we really going? Shall we *see* you sing again? We meant to hear you, even at home, but seeing's much better!"

"I should have thought you'd have heard quite enough of me lately. We'll all go together in the car. Just one thing, to please me, Lindy Bellanne! Don't chatter on the way home. I'm always so limp and tired."

"Oh, but I shan't want to talk. I shall be thinking it over and hearing the music."

Maidlin gave her a quick look; but it was no time to question her about her ambitions. "I'm glad you're so keen on music."

"Well, who wouldn't be, living here with you?"

Maidlin smiled. "Then you won't tire me with comments on the performance. And going up to town I shall be nervous; oh, yes, I'm always nervous till I start! Go and ask Nan if she'll come."

" But oughtn't we to stay here to help while you're out?"

" Mary can manage. She wants you to go. Both you and Mistress Bellanne have been working so hard for us. The twins will listen-in; they're very keen. So they'll be all right."

" Then thanks a million times!"

" Don't thank me! It was Doctor Robertson's idea."

" Doc-Jock?" Lindy sparkled.

" If you like. He gave me the tickets and asked if I wouldn't like to bring my visitors. I said I'd just love to bring the cook and the nursery governess."

Lindy laughed. " How simply marvellous of him to think of it!"

" It was kind," Maidlin agreed. " It was very like him. He often does that sort of thing."

It seemed to Anne that the wistful pleading in Maidlin's voice was stronger than ever, as she sang her great solo in the vast, tensely-listening hall. Lindy sat in rapt enjoyment of the music, but Anne's mind was busy asking: " What is it she wants? She's looking for something; she's seeking rest of some sort, and the craving has found its expression in her voice. She's singing magnificently; she'll have a storm of applause. Is it the older man she wants? She doesn't know it herself, of course. How will he wake her up to it? I'm sure she's wanting something."

Then came a great moment, for the soloists were sent for to the Royal Box, and Maidlin, with no time to be nervous, made her beautiful curtsey to the Queen, and was thanked for the great message she had given out so wonderfully.

She told Lindy and Anne about it as they drove home. "The Queen sent for us afterwards. She was lovely, and so kind. I'm proud to have spoken to her, for Rosamund has been presented at Court and has told me about it. She'll be thrilled to hear I've met the Queen too."

"You met a Princess when you were the May Queen at school, didn't you? Mary told me the story," Lindy said eagerly.

Maidlin smiled wearily. "That was a dreadful ordeal. It seems a long while ago. Now I've given you enough to think about, Lindy. Let me be quiet and rest."

"Nan can think about the Queen. I shall dream of *Elijah*. Those marvellous choruses!"

"Yes, they are wonderful," Maidlin assented.

"I never heard you sing that great solo quite as you did to-night," Anne ventured a word before they lapsed into silence.

Maidlin smiled at her. "That's what Dr. Jock said. I don't know why. It seemed just the same as usual to me."

She lay back in her corner, and the others took the hint and were silent, each with plenty to turn over in her mind. But it was not Elijah and the Prophets of Baal who haunted Maidlin that night, but the kind eyes of the man who had smiled at her, the special smile which he seemed to keep for concerts and for her, as he raised his baton for the music to begin. And afterwards, as he led her to the Queen, there had been something in his face

which she had seen before and had always taken
to mean that she had sung well.

"I think he was pleased." She curled up in bed
happily, after the supper and congratulations which
Mary had ready. "And that matters more than
the audience, or even the Queen, for it means he'll
use me again. I'm glad he seemed satisfied."

With her morning tea Mary brought a letter.

"From Donald!" Maidlin stared at it. "How
odd! Why didn't he say it last night, whatever
it is?"

She drank her tea thoughtfully, still looking at
the letter, while Mary, a little anxious, asked questions about the Queen and the concert, and told of
the comments of the twins.

"I suppose their measles, if any, will be our
next excitement." Maidlin sighed. "It's rather
weighing on us now, isn't it? We'll know by
Monday. I'll be glad to have it over."

It seemed likely to Mary that there was a still
more imminent excitement and that the unopened
letter in Maidlin's hand held the clue to it. She
took the tray, and Maidlin sighed again and opened
the envelope.

"What does this boy want now? He knows the
children can't go out with him at present."

Mary carried away the tray and was closing the
door when Maidlin called her. "Mary-Dorothy!"

At the startled note of alarm in her voice Mary
set down the tray and went back quickly into the
pink bedroom, closing the door. "Maid, dear,
what is it?"

"Donald wants to come—he's coming this afternoon—to see me. He doesn't want the twins, or you, or Lindy; just me. He says his uncle wouldn't let him come till after the concert. What do you suppose he means?''

Mary sat on the bed and gazed at her. '' Maid, don't you *know* what he means—what he wants?''

Maidlin lay and stared up at her, and slowly her pale cheeks grew red. '' You think—you mean he's going to—oh *no*, Mary! No! He couldn't be so silly!'' Her great dark eyes were larger than ever in her burning face.

'' It doesn't seem silly to him,'' Mary said stoutly, crushing down the anxiety in her heart. '' It's silly to me; you're far too good for a boy like Donald Robertson. But he doesn't think he's just a boy. He wants you, Maid. You'll need to tell him he can't have you.''

'' Donald! I never thought of it!'' Maidlin gasped. '' Oh—not *Donald*!''

A sudden wild torrent of sobbing shook her and she buried her head in her pillows. '' Mary, go away! Oh, please!''

'' But it's not so very dreadful, Maid.'' Mary pleaded, an arm thrown round her. '' We'll tell him you can't see him to-day, and then you can write. And I may be wrong about it—though I don't think I am. Don't cry like that, Maid, dear! He thinks he loves you, but he's only a boy—he'll get over it. You mustn't let it upset you, Maid.''

'' It's not that.'' Maidlin shook. '' I can't tell you, Mary. Please—oh, *please* go away! I don't care about Donald. It's—something else. I hadn't understood till you said Donald wanted—*Donald*! Oh, Mary, please go *away*!"

With deeply thoughtful eyes Mary rose. " Maid, dear, I'll leave you for half an hour. Lock your door so that the children can't come in; they're in a hurry to hear about the Queen. I'll keep them away; you shan't be disturbed. But when I come back, let me in, Maid, dear. There's something I want to say when you're ready to hear it. Don't keep me locked out, Maid. Joy wouldn't like you to do that."

" I want Joy! Oh, I want Joy!" Maidlin moaned.

" We all want Joy. But we have to be brave and see this through without her. Maid, dear, it's very hard on *me*. You'll see that when you think it over." She took Maidlin's hand and kissed it, and then left her alone.

" Hard on me!" she said to herself. " It's a great deal worse for Maid herself. But she's such a brick; I believe I used the only argument that she'd have listened to. She'll be sorry for me presently, and she'll let me in. I believe I can help her. I'd ring up Rosamund and ask her to come over, but Ros can't go near infection now that she has her baby. And I'm not sure that Maid would be pleased. She's given herself away to me, and she'll know it, but she won't expect me to say anything to anybody else."

She went to cope with the twins and to enlist Lindy's help in keeping them from Maidlin's room, saying that Aunty Maid was tired and they must wait.

In half an hour, badly frightened but quite determined, she tapped on Maidlin's door.

" Maid, dear, let me in. To please Joy, Maid,"
she pleaded.

She tried the handle and it turned easily. She
entered and stood staring round.

The room was empty. Looking very grave, Mary
closed the door and went downstairs.

CHAPTER XIII

THE MONKS' PATH

" Miss Maid? I saw her go across the garden,"
Anne said. " She was wearing her red cap and
jumper, and she had a stick. It seemed early to
go for a walk."

" Did she go to the Abbey?"

" No, the other way, towards the Manor."

" Nan, don't tell Lindy, or anybody. Maid's
had a letter that has upset her and she's gone out
because I said I was coming to talk to her. Let the
children think she's still resting," Mary pleaded.

Anne gave her a quick look. " What has happened?"

" I hardly know. I shall go after her; I think
I know where she'll be. She's had no breakfast,"
and Mary packed a satchel with sandwiches, an
apple, and a flask of hot coffee. " I had mine early;
I'm all right."

Anne watched her wistfully, and then came to
help. " You can't tell me any more?"

"Not yet. Don't ask me, Nan! It isn't fair to her."

Anne nodded regretfully. "Well, remember I'm just dying to hear the next chapter of Miss Maid's romance!"

"The next chapter is that young Donald wants to see her alone this afternoon," Mary said tersely. "For some reason it has thrown Maid right off her balance, or she wouldn't have run away from me. She's terribly upset. Just why, I can't tell you."

"Oh, but if—oh, well, all right." Anne swallowed her comment. "Make her be sensible, Mary!"

"I'm going to try." Mary went up to change into stout shoes. "I'll do my best, but it's a ticklish job."

She slung the satchel on her shoulder, took a stick, and set out for the hills.

The fact that Maidlin had carried a stick had given Mary the clue to her intention. She would not have done it if she had been going merely into the grounds of the deserted Manor. She had been making for the hills, and Mary thought she knew where she would find her.

The way was as straight as if marked with a ruler —the old Monks' Path, leading directly to the Abbey. A flight of moss-grown steps led steeply up the hill; a gate and a gap in the hedge showed where to cross the main road, and the white chalky track ran up the hill, crossed the winding road again, and went on and up, to end at last in a quarry, where a holy man of old had dug a little cell in which to pray and meditate.

Mary had nearly reached the quarry, climbing slowly, when Maidlin came running to meet her.

" Mary-Dorothy! Oh, Mary—all this way! Oh, what a brute I am! You must be dead—and carrying a bag! Oh, Mary, dear, why did you do it?"

" Pouf! What a climb! Where's your monk's cell? I want to rest. This is your breakfast, Maid."

" Oh—Mary!" Maidlin wailed. " I could cry with shame! I hadn't run away, Mary—not really. It was just that I wasn't ready to talk. Mary-Dorothy, can you forgive me?"

" If you eat that breakfast while I rest, I'll never tell anybody that you ran away," Mary said solemnly.

" Not Jen? Or Rosamund?" Maidlin begged. " Don't give me away, Mary! You must share this food; there's too much for me, and you've had all that climb. You are a dear! I'd just remembered I'd had nothing to eat."

" I knew you'd be starving when you did remember," Mary assented. She sat looking down on the wide view: the Abbey, the Hall, and the Manor among their trees; the village with its white roads, and all the stretch of green country fading into blue distance. " I haven't been up here often. What a place for prayer and meditation! And the straight track running down to the Abbey. It's wonderful."

She accepted coffee and sandwiches, and throwing off her hat enjoyed the bracing wind and the sunshine.

" Mary, do you understand?" Maidlin asked abruptly.

" No. But I know you'll tell me as much as you can."

Maidlin turned to her impetuously. " It's dreadful for you, as you said, to have me going on like this! I ought to be a help to you instead of a worry."

" It's much worse than the twins and their measles," Mary said simply. " I can have doctors and nurses for the children, but no one can help me in this mess but you. And with you suddenly going all artist and Italian, I feel a bit frightened, Maid."

Maidlin laid a hand on her knee. " Mary, I am sorry! I'll do what I can to make up. It isn't Donald, Mary. I'm not in the least upset about him." She looked at Mary bravely and honestly, but her eyes shrank and her cheeks were crimson.

Mary's hand closed over hers. " Maid, dear, I'd give everything I have to bring Joy to you at this moment. But as I can't do it, you must let me try to help. Donald's letter told you something you hadn't realised quite clearly; was that it?"

" Something I'd never dreamt of!" Maidlin said vehemently. " It was as if he'd hit me in the face. I knew I could never marry him, because——" Her voice broke, and she turned from Mary, but without drawing away her hand.

Mary summoned up all her courage. " You can push me off the quarry, if you feel like it, and I shall roll right down on to the roof of the Abbey. I'm sure I couldn't stop myself. Maid, you can't marry Donald because there's somebody else you could marry. That's why the letter upset you so much."

" I didn't know!" Maidlin cried, and snatched away her hand and covered her face. " I'd never dreamt of it. And he doesn't feel like that in the least. I ought not—oh, Mary! What can I do? He doesn't care; I'm only a nice voice for his concerts."

" But what makes you think that?" Mary demanded, her tone as matter-of-fact as she could make it.

" He's never said anything. He never comes here. He lets Donald come; he sends music and messages by Donald. I'm only an addition to his orchestra; not a person at all."

" I don't believe it. When he came to see the Abbey there was something more than that in his face as he said good-bye to you," Mary exclaimed. " Maid, be honest! You may feel just now that it has been a mistake, but haven't you seen something in him to make you think of him like this?"

" I've never thought of it," Maidlin cried. " I haven't been thinking of him, or Donald, in that way. He's always kind, but that's all. And I've wondered lately why he never came here."

Mary nodded thoughtfully. " That's like you. It wouldn't occur to you that a man might be falling in love with you."

Maidlin turned startled eyes on her. " I'm quite certain he isn't! Mary, how can you?"

" Well, I'm not certain," Mary asserted. " You'll say I'm spinning romances, as Jen did, when I told her that Kenneth loved her. You know how right I was about that. Maid, may I tell you this story as I see it?"

Maidlin nodded, her head bent. "But I won't promise to believe you. You do make up stories, you know, Mary."

"Suppose Dr. Robertson liked you very much —we'll put it that way"—as Maidlin quivered in distress—"and then young Donald turned up, home from his visit to South Africa. You and Donald make such a nice couple; any one can see that! So the older man says to himself: 'I must stand back and let this youngster have his chance. He's her age, and he ought to be her mate. I can't butt in and spoil things for them.' Don't you think that's possible?"

Maidlin was staring at her. "But he couldn't think I'd marry a boy like Donald!"

"He could, very well. It looks so obvious. Dr. Robertson doesn't know about your grown-up side; he may suspect it, but I imagine you haven't shown him your whole self—except in your singing, of course."

"He must look on me as a baby," Maidlin said slowly.

"Now's your chance to prove to him that you're not."

Maidlin turned wide dark eyes upon her again. "How, Mary? What can I do?"

"See Donald—be brave—tell him to go away— and then wait and see what happens."

"What do you think will happen?" Maidlin demanded.

"If I'm right about Dr. Robertson, when he hears Donald's news, he'll come to ask you what it means. In any case he'll know he has been mistaken about Donald and you. I believe he's been sacrificing himself and standing back to find out whether you really wanted Donald. It's what any decent older man would do.''

'' He's not old!'' Maidlin cried. '' He's younger than Ivor; he's frightfully young to be a Doctor of Music. He's only ten years older than I am.''

'' That's about right, for you,'' Mary said thoughtfully. '' It was right for Jen to marry a man only a little older than herself; it was right for Rosamund to marry a delicate man who must always need her care; but for you, it must be a man you can look up to and lean upon. Yes, it's right in each case.''

Maidlin, crimson, gazed at her. '' It's too soon to talk of marrying. But I'd never want a boy like Donald.''

'' No, you're older than he is in many ways. Well, Maid, you have your chance now to be brave and fight for your own man and win him.''

'' Mary!'' Maidlin gasped.

'' I mean it. You can't funk this interview with Donald. It may be the turning-point of your life. If I'm right, it's the only way to show Dr. Robertson that he's wrong.''

'' And just suppose ''—Maidlin's laugh was overwrought and hysterical—'' that you're wrong all through, Mary-Dorothy, and when Donald comes this afternoon he just suggests another picnic or brings more music and roses!''

'' I don't think so. But if that happens, we'll forget all this and wait.''

'' It's a lot to forget! Mary, would you go for

a walk on the hill and leave me to think some more?''

Mary swept the remains of the breakfast into her bag. '' I shall go home and get on with my work. Those proofs must be posted to-day. You'll come when you're ready.''

'' You are a dear, Mary-Dorothy!'' Maidlin said gratefully, and sat clasping her knees and watching Mary as she went carefully down the steep path.

Then she picked up her stick and turned to wander on the hills.

CHAPTER XIV

A LARK SINGS IN THE ABBEY

'' LET'S go into your old Abbey place, shall we?'' Donald Robertson cried gaily, as he slammed the door of his car.

'' No, not the Abbey. Come into the garden.'' Maidlin's turning from the Abbey would have warned him, if he had known her better. '' Lindy and the twins are having school in there,'' she added. '' We're making up for lost time by having morning and afternoon school, and the children are completely thrilled. It's almost all play, of course, but they don't realise that.''

And, looking grave but not showing how frightened she felt, she led him towards a summer-house in a quiet corner of the garden.

Ten minutes later Donald came striding back, his

face white and indignant, sprang into the car and was gone.

Maidlin was white too as she turned into the Abbey path. It had not been easy to convince Donald, and she had felt sore for his sake. She had made him believe she was in earnest; that had been necessary, if the result Mary had hinted at was to follow; he had been incredulous at first; then, realising the truth, had been inexcusably angry.

" Didn't you know what I was after?" he demanded.

" Not for a second." Maidlin's temper blazed up. " I don't go about thinking people are wanting to marry me! You were kind; we all enjoyed your picnics, but they meant no more to me than to any of the others. I'm sorry, Donald, but it's not a scrap of use."

Her anger had died down quickly, for he was obviously much distressed; but she was tired out, and when he went she turned to the Abbey for comfort. There were quiet corners where Lindy and the twins would not see her. The age-long peace of the ruins would bring healing and rest.

As she went through the Abbot's garden, the ancient peace was broken, and Maidlin stood as if turned to stone. " Who is it? Who can be in the Abbey?"

Someone was singing, in a clear high soprano, untrained but very sweet and strong. It was an old nursery song, and it broke off suddenly in the middle.

" I can't get that bit right. Tell me once more, Twins!"

Elizabeth and Margaret chanted the last phrases in unison, and the soprano rang out again, correctly this time.

Maidlin, with dazed, unbelieving eyes, crept down the shadowy tresaunt passage and stood in the dark entrance.

The twins, perched on low forms, were gazing up at Lindy, as she sang the nursery rhyme. There was no one else in the Abbey.

Margaret flopped on the grass. " Now, Aunty Lin, sing us about ' The Fox and the Grapes,' while we have a rest."

" And why don't I need a rest too?"

" Oh, you're big! You can always go on singing." Elizabeth curled up against her. " Go on, Miss Belinda! Twin f'got we was at school."

" Lindy Bellanne, why didn't you tell me?" Maidlin came out from the shadows.

Lindy sprang to her feet, her face crimson. " Oh, Miss Maid! You heard?"

" I heard you singing. How have you managed to keep that voice a secret for so long?"

Lindy's eyes sought hers, confused and shy. " I came into the Abbey when you were in town or if I knew you were out. I had to sing sometimes."

" Of course you had. Is that what you want to be—a singer?"

" I'm dying to have good training!" Lindy broke out. " I love singing more than anything, but what's the use? We can't afford it. Nan's sure and certain we can't. I want *good* lessons, you know."

" You want the best," Maidlin said, eyeing her

with keen professional interest, for in Lindy's voice
and manner there was a quality of dramatic in-
tensity, born of her great eagerness, which, Maidlin
thought, might be trained to wide uses. Opera?
Was Belinda Bellanne the operatic singer that she
herself had refused to be, thereby disappointing
Ivor Quellyn, who felt her voice was not being
given its full expression on the concert platform?
Would all the great soprano roles be open to Lindy
one day? Time would show; she must certainly
be trained.

"How I'd love to present her to Ivor, and
say, 'Here's your opera singer—a dramatic
soprano '!" she thought.

Lindy's eyes were on her wistfully. "I
couldn't tell you," she pleaded. "With your
lovely, marvellous voice, and all your big success,
how could I pipe up and say, 'I want to sing
too '? It would have seemed too feeble."

"There's nothing feeble about your voice,"
Maidlin exclaimed. "So you sing to the twinnies
as part of their lessons?"

"If you're out," Lindy said ruefully. "We
thought you were going out in Mr. Donald's car."

Maidlin flushed, but swept Donald Robertson
aside. "He had to go, quite quickly. Twins, why
didn't you tell me Aunt Lindy could sing?"

"Told us not to. And she's Miss Belinda. It's
school," said Elizabeth.

"And you're interruptin', Aunty Maid," Margaret added severely. "Twin and me wants to
hear about the Fox."

"I'll listen too." Maidlin took half of Elizabeth's

cushion and squatted on the grass. " Now, Belinda Bellanne—what a name for the posters!—this is the Albert Hall; the twins are the ten thousand people and I'm the Queen. Tell us about the Fox and the Grapes!"

" Oh, how can I? I should die!" Lindy protested.

" Not you; not with that voice. However shy you are, you really want to use it. Do you think I don't know? Fire away!"

" Fire away, Miss Belinda!" the twins chuckled together.

Lindy gulped, looked across the garth at the windows of the chapter-house, and plunged into the fable.

Maidlin gazed up at her, amazed. The refrain, with its " Tra-la-la," suited Lindy's voice, and already the strength of her singing was surprising. What would she not be able to make of trills and shakes and lark-notes when she had been thoroughly trained?

" But you've been well taught already!" she exclaimed, as the twins broke into applause.

" Only at school. The man who came for singing was rather keen on me."

" I can believe it! Well, Twins, I'm afraid that's the end of Miss Belinda, the nursery governess. And it seemed such a jolly plan!"

" Oh, but why?" Lindy cried. " I want to stay with them!"

" You're not goin' away!" Margaret shouted. " You can't go away now!"

" All our aunties go away!" Elizabeth mourned.

" Aunty Gail and Aunty Benedicta, and now you say Aunt Lindy too. Why can't she stay?"

" I didn't say she must go away. But she has other things to do; she won't have time for nursery lessons. Lindy, have you heard that we have a Music School in the village here?"

Lindy's eyes widened. " A Music School? What's that? We don't know anything about the village."

" No, thanks to the measles. There are lots of things that you haven't heard of yet—country-dance classes that I'm supposed to teach, and my Camp Fire Girls, and Mary's Sunday School. We've had to take a holiday from all sorts of things because of the risk of infection."

" And it's been all no use," Lindy said incautiously. " Pity you fagged to quarantine yourselves!"

" Why no use?" Margaret asked instantly.

Maidlin looked at Lindy, who reddened in dismay. " Oh, I say! I'm sorry, Miss Maid."

" Why are you sorry? What d'you mean?" Elizabeth demanded, scenting something between Lindy and Maidlin which had not been explained. " Tell us, Aunty Maid!"

" Presently, 'Lisbeth! I want to tell Miss Belinda about the Music School. That's where she must go, so she ought to hear about it."

" Oh yes, tell her! But you ought to tell her in the talking-place, and that's the parlour," Margaret said reproachfully. " And you said she couldn't be Miss Belinda any more."

" This is much nicer, out in the sun. Perhaps

she could make time to be Miss Belinda for a little while each morning.'' Maidlin smiled at Lindy.

'' Me and Twin like our new schoolroom,'' Elizabeth urged. '' We don't want her to go away.''

'' The Music School was started by Joy, to help girls who wanted to go in for music but had difficulty in getting the proper training,'' Maidlin began.

Lindy sank on a cushion. '' What a marvellous idea! What made her do it?''

'' There was a time when she was restless and unhappy because music was working inside her and she had no one to help her to bring it out. You know what lovely little songs she writes now; she used to try to compose, as a girl, but she hadn't had enough training. When she inherited the Hall and was able to do anything she wanted, that was one of her plans; to have a Music School and help girls who felt as she did. You must go to the school, Lindy Bellanne; you're exactly the sort of girl it's meant for. You'll have good lessons; visiting masters come, or girls go in to Oxford or to London. You'll work and you'll practise. I think you should aim at a scholarship to the Royal College of Music, but that will be decided for you later. You'll have your chance, and with that voice you're sure to make good. In a few years you'll be a singer, and, if your voice improves as it should do, a great singer. There's your future settled, Miss Belinda!''

'' It sounds too marvellous for words.'' There was a touch of awe in Lindy's tone.

'' You'll have to work; you've a long way to go. But you'll love every minute of the work. I know all about it." Maidlin smiled at her. " I've been trained and watched over so carefully. I didn't understand at the time, but I appreciate it now. I shall tell Joy about you. She'll be thrilled; she does so love to help the right people!"

" But she doesn't know me! Why should she do so much for me? Ought I to let her? Is it right for me to take my whole training from somebody? I can't ever hope to repay her," Lindy faltered.

" Oh, I can't agree! You'll repay her when you're a great singer. She often says I repay her for all the trouble she took over me. That's the repayment she wants—that you make good and use the training she'll give you."

" I'll do it!" Lindy vowed.

" You'd have to use that voice, you know. Some day you'll sing the lark songs and send your notes ringing out and up and down as the lark does. Those aren't for me, of course. Perhaps some day you and I will sing together in the quartets of *Elijah*, Lindy Bellanne!"

Lindy looked at her, wide-eyed and incredulous. " I could *never* be good enough for that!"

" Oh yes, you could. You will be! And the lovely soprano parts—' Rejoice Greatly ' and ' I Know that my Redeemer Liveth ' and the others; all for you!"

" I *never* could!" Lindy whispered again, her tone full of awe.

" Of course you could. Shall we go and tell your sister?"

" But it's still school!" Margaret protested.

" Aunty Maid, you have been an int'ruption to-day!"

Maidlin smiled at Lindy. " Then I must apologise to Miss Belinda. But I was coming down the tresaunt when she began to sing, and I came to look for the lark in the Abbey."

" The lark in the Abbey!" Elizabeth chuckled. " That's a nice name for her!"

" Why didn't you go out with Uncle Don?" Margaret grumbled. " Then we'd have had our lessons."

" Where were you going in the Abbey?" Elizabeth demanded. " Couldn't you go there now, and let us do some work?"

" Oh, Elizabeth!" Maidlin laughed. " I'm ticked off, Lindy. Yes, I'll go and let you do your work. I was going to sit in the sacristy. May I have one of your cushions?"

" Why were you? It's dull in there. Nothing to do in the sacristy," Elizabeth argued.

" It's not nearly so dull as the parlour you're so fond of!"

" But the parlour's the talking-place!" Margaret cried.

" And you like talking," Maidlin agreed. " The sacristy was a favourite place of your mother's, Twinnies. That's why I want to sit there."

" To think about Mother?" The twins eyed her curiously.

" Exactly." Maidlin picked up a scarlet cushion.

" Why?" they asked breathlessly, both together.

" Isn't Mother a nice thing to think about?"

" Yes. We'll come and think about her too!"
They gave a united shout.

" Oh no, you won't! A lot of thinking I should
do, if you were there. You can think about her some
other time. Just now you're in school, and Miss
Belinda's waiting," Maidlin said firmly. " You'd
better make the most of her while she's here. Soon
she'll go to live at the Music School and you'll have
to do without her."

The twins hurled themselves on Lindy. " Don't
do it! Don't go to that old school! You can learn
singing here. Aunty Maid can teach you. We want
you to go on being our Miss Belinda."

Lindy's eyes were like stars, with the new hopes
that had been flung before her. But she held herself in tightly and turned her mind rigidly to the
duty of the moment, as Maidlin, seeing her condition, had intended she should do.

" We'll have some drill and marching, Twins.
Fetch your wands and we'll do those new exer-
cises."

Maidlin nodded approval, and went through the
gap in the wall and round the corner to the little
vestry, where Joy had once been wont to sit in the
empty rose window. The garth rang with Lindy's
words of command, and the twins raised and
lowered their wands energetically and rhythmic-
ally, and there was no one to tell them that it was
with a drill class on the garth the story of the Abbey
Girls had begun, so many years ago.

CHAPTER XV

MAIDLIN MEETS ADVENTURE

MAIDLIN, sitting in the rose window, roused herself with a shake of dismay. She had not been thinking of Joy, nor of Lindy and her career, nor of Donald's disappointment. All sorts of little things had come crowding upon her, in the light of Mary's suggestion. Happy in her music and the certainty of Dr. Jock's friendship and approval, she had not given a thought to the future or to anything deeper than the pleasure of the moment, but now she kept remembering small forgotten details—his kindly eyes as he smiled at her from the conductor's desk, the clasp of his hand as he led her to the Queen, his tone as he said good-night and put her into the car with Anne and Lindy; and earlier things—a glance, a word, which had meant nothing at the time; his appreciation of the Abbey, which had pleased her so much; his gentleness with the twins after the accident in the tree; and—if Mary were right—his standing back to give her a fair chance to decide between himself and Donald.

" It was for me, so that I shouldn't be hurried; not for Donald. He was giving me the chance to have Donald if I wanted him. He's always kind—and fair. But is Mary right? Or is it just a story she's made up?"

She sprang to her feet at last. " This won't do! I have to wait and see. I must make myself forget.

Of course! We must tell Anne Bellanne that I know her sister's secret.''

She found the garth empty. Lindy and the children had finished school for the day and had gone home to tea.

Maidlin, hurrying after them, found Lindy waiting for her on the terrace. '' I want to tell Nan. May I, Miss Maid? She's been telling me to explain to you, ever since we came here.'' Her face was radiant with joy and excitement.

'' Jolly sensible of her. You were a silly kid to try to keep that voice dark. Let's tell her together.''

'' Oh, good!'' Lindy caught her hand and they ran to the kitchen.

'' Nan! Oh, Nan! I've told her! I mean, she found out!'' Lindy shouted. '' And I have been an idiot, as you said.''

Anne looked at them over her pastry-board, her sleeves rolled up and her hands in a big bowl. She had been hoping for news from, or of, Maidlin, but not this news, and she was taken by surprise.

'' Oh? You've come to your senses at last, then?''

'' She heard me singing with the twins. I thought she'd gone out with Mr. Donald.''

Anne's eyes flashed to Maidlin's and caught a gleam in them which told her everything, or at least a good deal. '' She won't go out with Mr. Donald again,'' she said to herself.

'' Nan, her voice is going to be lovely,'' Maidlin cried. '' I couldn't believe my ears when I heard a skylark singing in our Abbey!''

Lindy laughed happily and perched herself on

the corner of the table, her yellow curls falling on her cheeks as she bent over a bowl of raisins. "May I steal one? Nan, it's just too marvellous for words!" and she plunged into the story of Joy's Music School and the plans for her own training.

"But I don't want to leave the twins," and she looked anxiously at Maidlin. "You do need me here, don't you? I've been a help, haven't I?"

"An enormous help already, and if they should be ill you're going to be invaluable," Maidlin said warmly. "If you could bear to postpone your training for a few months, and put up with lessons from me, just for a start, then I think you should stay and help us till Joy comes home and makes new plans, or till Cecily can come from Switzerland and live here for a time. She could take on your job; her French and music are perfect. But we can't have her just now, so we do really need you badly."

"I'll love to stay! And if you would—but it isn't fair. You have your own music to attend to."

"I can help you a good deal," Maidlin said. "It will all be useful when you begin in earnest. Will you wait a little while before going back to school?"

"Oh, rather! I could dance with joy!"

"You will dance, if you stay here, once this quarantine is over," Maidlin informed her. "You'll come to my country-dance class; nothing could be better for your music. All kinds of music will be useful for you. I hope Anne Bellanne will come too. We have good times; everybody enjoys it."

"You are being the Good Angel of the Bell-annes!" Anne exclaimed. "I'm more grateful than I can say for all these kind plans for Lindy."

"It will be a joy to help her to use her voice. It's going to be really good, Nan," Maidlin said earnestly. "I feel she's my discovery; I never found a voice before! I'm thrilled and proud. It's going to be a real privilege to turn her into a singer —an adventure for both of us!"

"Some day we're going to sing in *Elijah* together, in the Albert Hall!" Lindy gave an exultant shout. "I shall be the leading soprano and Miss Maid will be the contralto to back me up!"

Anne gave Maidlin a look of wordless gratitude. "This is going to alter Lindy. There'll be no more trouble with her. It will remake her whole life," she said to herself. "The very least I can do for Miss Maid is to leave her alone just now, when I fancy she's in rather deep waters, and not ask questions. She mustn't guess I've noticed anything. I meant to go to Mary's room to-night, to see if she'd tell me anything, but I'll not do it. We shall hear in time; we're still very new friends."

To Mary's surprise and immense relief no questions were asked, and Anne did not hint at the curiosity that was filling her. No reference was made to Donald's brief visit. The news of Lindy's career filled every one's surface thoughts and their deeper ones remained hidden. Maidlin went to the piano and sang Joy's songs, and Lindy was coaxed into singing some things she had learned at school.

"We'll give you your first lesson to-morrow." Maidlin smiled up at her from the piano. "There are a lot of things I want to tell you, so that you can begin to work in earnest. You must have regular times for practice, as I do. The twins will have to be content with rather less of Miss Belinda, but they'll be so glad to know they're going to keep you that they'll put up with it."

" I shall never want to go away from them," Lindy said earnestly.

Her first lesson was a great delight. As Miss Belinda she took the children to school in the Abbey and taught and played with them for two hours; then, at eleven o'clock, she brought them back to the house for milk and biscuits, left them in Mary's care, and went to Maidlin, who was sitting at Joy's beautiful piano.

The time went quickly, unnoticed by both. Half an hour later the twins came dancing in, clamouring to be allowed to share in the lesson.

" We've done our writing with Aunt Mary. Our copies were jolly good; she said so. Now can't we have some singing?" Elizabeth leaned on the piano.

" I can sing like Aunty Lin!" Margaret shouted. " Tra-la-la! I can do it too!"

" You! You only shriek," Lindy teased.

" All sing this little song together," Maidlin suggested. " You know it, Twinnies. Aunty Lin will lead. Now off you go—' 'Twas on a Monday morning.' Ready?"

" Washing day. We know it," Margaret cried, and threw back her head and clasped her hands behind her and prepared to shout.

" You'll spoil it, silly girl," Elizabeth protested. " Too loud isn't nice, is it, Aunty Maid?"

" No, it's horrid, and it's bad singing," Maidlin said severely. " Margaret mustn't do more than her share, or we won't have her in our choir."

Margaret giggled. " All right, I won't. I was goin' to sing loudest, louder than Aunty Lin."

" I know you were. I saw you," Elizabeth said indignantly. " I call that screaming, not singing."

Margaret subdued her energy to a decent pitch and the gay song filled the hall, Lindy's full rich notes leading the shriller piping of the twins.

" But this voice shows great promise! She must be trained——"

The singers whirled round. Maidlin looked up, only one part of her surprised. In her heart she had known he would come to-day.

" Aunty Maid, it's a man," cried Margaret.

" He came before, when Twin was the kitten in the beashly tree," Elizabeth added.

Lindy had heard Dr. Robertson's words and could only gaze at him, startled and happy.

" Forgive me!" He smiled down at Maidlin. " I was going to knock at the door and be a proper visitor, but I heard the singing and I'm afraid I forgot and walked right in. This is the little friend whom I saw at the Albert Hall, isn't it? But don't you know how good her voice is?"

" Or will be, when it's trained." Maidlin smiled at Lindy. " Oh yes, I know! But I only discovered her secret yesterday. She never told me she wanted to sing. We have all sorts of plans for her future. Some day she's going to be leading soprano in the Albert Hall and I'll be her humble second. She has plenty of time; she's only just left school."

" I apologise. Of course you would know the value of her voice. May I hear something else? And could these two be part of the audience with me?" he suggested.

" Want to hear Aunty Lin sing alone?" Margaret asked shrewdly.

" What's your name?" Elizabeth took his hand and gazed up at him. " Uncle what? You won't send us away, will you? We want to hear too."

He laughed; no one could resist Elizabeth when she chose to plead.

" Uncle Jock. I teach people to sing, and I want to hear—what do you call your friend?"

" Aunt Lindy, or Aunty Lin."

" Or Miss Belinda, when it's lessons. She's Miss Belinda Bellanne," Margaret put in.

" A good name!" He smiled at Lindy. " Well, I want to hear her sing alone, but if you'll pretend to be the audience I'll let you stay. The audience is always very quiet, you know; they never whisper or wriggle about."

" I can be quiet when I like," Margaret said defiantly.

" We'll be the best audience there ever was." Elizabeth retreated to a big settle. " Come here quickly, Twin. They can't start till you're sitting down. The audience always sits down. We've been to concerts, Uncle Jock," she said, with dignity. " We know how to be a good audience."

His lips twitched, but he spoke seriously. " Show

us, then. Now, Miss Belinda Bellanne, let me hear you sing!"

"And don't be frightened. Sing as you did for me alone," Maidlin added.

"Yes!" he said, when Lindy, inwardly terrified, had done her best. "There's no doubt about your future, child. We'll help you to realise it. You're in good hands, for the moment," and he gave Maidlin a smile. "I won't butt in; she's your discovery. But I may be able to help later on. And now I want you to take me into your Abbey again. That's what I came to ask for. Will you come?"

Not the friendly "Miss Maid" she had grown used to, but "You." Maidlin looked up at him and read in his face all that he would presently say.

She bent over the keys for one moment. Then she looked up again, her heart in her eyes, and rose. "To the Abbey—yes, I'll come."

She went out and he followed. Lindy stared after them wide-eyed.

"We'll go too!" Margaret shouted, and darted to the door.

Lindy dashed after her and caught her. "No, you don't! They don't want an audience now! Come and find somebody! Oh, Mary-Dorothy! Nan! Dr. Jock's taken Miss Maid away into the Abbey, and—and she wanted to go!"

"Oh, I hope she'll be happy!" Mary whispered, and shut herself into her own room. "Maid's facing her great adventure, and she's leaping to grasp it, not hanging back as she's always done till now. But—oh, how I wish Joy was here!"

Anne came from the kitchen to help Lindy with

the twins. "Don't say anything to the maids, Lindy. Keep it to yourself."

"Does he want—will they get married?" Lindy whispered, one eye on the children.

"I think so. Mary and I have been hoping it would happen."

"Oh, you pigs! You might have told me! I thought it was Mr. Donald who was going to ask her."

Anne gave her a look. "Perhaps he did. But she didn't want him."

"Do you mean yesterday? Was that why he went away so soon?"

"I think so," Anne said again. "But she hasn't told me."

"Two days—two men—two proposals!" Lindy murmured. "Miss Maid's being kept busy! I like this one best, Nan."

"So does she, if she's gone with him into the Abbey."

"She said: 'To the Abbey—yes, I'll come.' And when she looked at him, and he looked at her, I knew, Nan."

"Don't say any more. Wait for her to tell us. Twins!" Anne called to the children, who were strumming out a duet on the piano. "I thought you weren't allowed to do that?"

"Oh, well!" Elizabeth wriggled off the stool. "Can't we go in the Abbey too?"

"I'm going into the garden to fetch some rhubarb. Who's coming with me?"

"We are, if we can't go in the Abbey with new

Uncle Jock," Elizabeth said sadly. "He's awful nice!"

"I s'pose you and the rhubarb will be better than nothing," Margaret added. "Can I carry the big leaves and throw them into the pit?"

"You shall," Anne promised, and led the way.

CHAPTER XVI

TELLING ROSAMUND

"MARY! Mary-Dorothy!" The big door was thrown open and Maidlin sent her call ringing through the house.

Mary came running from her room. "Yes, Maid? You've not been long. The others are in the garden."

"A party of Americans arrived, and we fled." Maidlin's voice trembled between laughter and tears. "Am I needed here, Mary? Could you spare me for to-day? I—we want to go out in—in Jock's car. Oh, Mary, you were right! It wasn't just romancing; it was true!"

Mary gazed at her, a new Maidlin she had never seen before, changed, lit up by some great new thing within her. "Oh, Maid, my dear!"

Maidlin ran into her arms and clung to her. "Mary, you cheered me up. Thank you; you did help. And you knew; you understood him. It was just what you said. I told him, and he said you'd been a brick. He wants to thank you; but not now. He's getting the car ready; I came for my coat.

He says I'm to wear my red cap—fancy caring what I wear! Mary, will you tell Nan and Lindy? And the children, of course. They'll understand. You don't mind if I go? I don't know when I'll be back!"

"Run along and be happy, Maid dear. I am so very thankful!" Mary ran upstairs with her to put her into her coat and to find the red cap. "He'll take care of you!"

"Oh yes!" Maidlin said happily. "Everything's all right now! But we've so much to say, and those Americans—we just ran away! Jock said: 'I've got the car here. We'll fly from everybody.' And I said I'd like that."

Then she was gone, waving good-bye to Mary on the terrace.

Mary drew a long breath of relief and went to meet the party in the garden.

"Where are we going?" Maidlin asked presently, as the car sped along the white roads.

Jock Robertson smiled down at her. "I've no idea. It's for you to say. We're running away from the tourists; that's all I know. Except that we took the road to the south. You always make me think of the south."

"Oh, but half of me belongs to the north. You'll have to see my farm in Cumberland, where I was brought up."

"I want to take you to Italy."

"Please don't! I've been to Italy so many times. But it would be different with you," she added.

"Well, what about Spain? Or Greece?"

" That would be fun. Jock, perhaps you'll laugh, but there's something I'd like to do now, at once."

He looked at her curiously, conscious that he had many discoveries to make, although he felt he knew her well.

" If it's possible we'll do it, Maid. I like to feel I may leave out the ' Miss ' at last!"

" It's odd how easy I find it to say ' Jock.' I thought I'd never dare," Maidlin said. " It isn't a hard thing I want—just to slip into an old church somewhere for five minutes and say thank you because I'm so happy. Are you going to laugh?"

" On the contrary, I'm coming with you. Do you think I'm less thankful than you are?"

" Oh, that will be nice! I'm glad you'll do it too," Maidlin exclaimed, heartfelt relief in her tone. " You see, I once asked for help when I needed it very badly; I'll tell you the story some time."

" And the help came?"

" At once, and all I wanted. Ever since then I've been thankful, and more than ever now."

" Ewelme is the place," Jock said. " I know this country fairly well. It's a lovely old church."

" And now where shall we go?" he asked, when the few quiet moments were over. " Isn't there anything else you want very badly?"

" There's one other thing, but it's too difficult."

" Tell me!" he urged.

" I want to tell Joy. She's like my mother; she ought to hear before any one else."

Jock pulled up the car, and took out a note-case

and counted the contents, while Maidlin watched with puzzled eyes.

" Plenty!" he announced. " You shall speak to Joy. She'll still be in bed; it's early morning in New York; but she can get up and come to the phone."

" Jock! You don't mean——?"

" Why not? What better use could there be for the transatlantic phone? If you're frightened I'll speak for you."

" Oh, I'm not! I've done it before; Joy once rang me up, and I heard her quite well. But I never thought—I didn't mean—isn't it frightfully expensive?"

" I must give you a present to-day. Isn't this what you'd like best?"

" Oh, you do understand!" Maidlin sighed happily. " Of course it is! To tell Joy myself—oh, Jock!"

" It will get into the papers. You're a celebrity and I'm not unknown." He gave her a schoolboy grin. " We must tell your Joy before she reads it in print."

" Oh, Jock—yes! Let's hurry!"

" My first gift to you; there will be plenty more of them. Now where shall we phone from? A village call-box is hardly adequate, I think."

" Not for New York." Maidlin laughed in excitement and delight. " This is a thrill! But won't it take a long while to get through?"

" Some time, I expect. Shall we run down to Brighton, have lunch, and ring up from there?"

" Oh, not Brighton! It's so big and crowded."

Maidlin knit her brows. " We ought to have done it from the Hall. Where are we, Jock?"

He pulled out a map. " Near the Thames at Wallingford. We've just passed through Watlington."

" Could we go on into Sussex?"

" Easily. Here goes!" He shoved the map away and the car shot forward. " Whereabouts in Sussex?"

" Kentisbury Castle. Rosamund would let us phone from there. And I can tell her, and that's the second thing I want to do—only second to telling Joy."

" Right! A clear programme. The Castle is the very place, and your Countess-chum ought to hear your news. I know what good pals you are."

" I met you first at the Castle, when I stayed with Ros and she asked you to dinner. I'd seen you before, but we hadn't met."

" I'd certainly seen you," Jock laughed. " I was at your first concert, when you sang the little story of Silvy, the highwayman. I said to myself: ' That's my girl; but she'd never have an old chap like me, ten years older than herself!' And when Donald appeared I was sure you'd pair off with him. You ought to have had him, you know. He fitted you so well."

" I was sorry for Donald," Maidlin began.

" He's young; he'll get over it. He's gone off, saying he'll go back to South Africa. His mother had warned him that it was no use, I believe; she says now she was sure you wouldn't marry him. But she didn't say it to me. I've had an idea! If young Donald comes back in four years or so, we'll marry him to your little soprano. She's about the right age for Don!''

" Lindy Bellanne!'' Maidlin laughed in delight. " Oh yes, Jock! They'd make a lovely couple. Her voice is going to be wonderful, so he'd have a singing girl, after all. I feel much more like Donald's mother or his aunt than——''

" Than his wife. Well, you'll be his aunt, so that's all right. But he won't like it, poor lad.''

" I wonder if I told him I'd rather be his aunt?'' Maidlin said reflectively. " I've no idea what I said. I hope I didn't!''

Jock threw back his head and shouted. " Maid! If you did——! The poor boy!''

" I didn't! I'm sure I didn't! He made me angry, but I don't believe I talked about aunts.''

" I hope you didn't! He knows now how I've been feeling for the last fortnight—thinking I'd lost you, you know. But I've told you all that already. I'll tell you another thing about your first concert. From that night, I wanted you for oratorio. I craved for your voice in ' He shall feed ' and ' He was despised ' and ' O rest.' *I* couldn't rest till I'd persuaded Ivor Quellyn that oratorio was your real place.''

" You understand me better than Ivor did, even then. He stormed at me because I wouldn't go into opera.''

" He told me; and I said he was wrong. You aren't dramatic. Oratorio's your place; I couldn't have you wasting your voice on concert songs.''

Jock's eyes were searching the roadsides, and

presently he drew up before an old barn, trans-
formed into an attractive tea-house.

" You must be fed. You'll like this place. Lady
Kentisbury will ask us to lunch; we must be able
to say we've had it."

" Oh yes! Just the two of us together," Maidlin
agreed happily. " What a fascinating spot! And
I'll choose the place for tea. I know where I want
to go."

An hour later the car crossed the drawbridge and
drew up in the green quadrangle of the Castle. A
phone call from the Tea-Barn had made sure that
the Countess would be at home, and she was waiting for them, full of curiosity as to the reason for
this sudden visit.

" Maid, why are you running about the country
with Dr. Robertson?" she asked severely.

" Ros! Oh, Ros! Don't you know why?"
Maidlin ran into her arms.

" I can guess." Rosamund stretched out one
hand to Jock while the other clasped Maidlin tightly
to her. " I won't say I saw it coming, but I've had
hopes. My dear, I'm so glad. Happy, Maid? I
can see *he* is."

" Oh—*yes*! I never dreamt it would be like
this," Maidlin whispered.

" You have gone all out for it," Rosamund
laughed, as she kissed her. " But, of course, it
had to be all or nothing with you! Maid, dear,
careers are all very well, and bringing up other
people's children is quite jolly, but you've reached
out and grasped the real thing, and I'm glad and
thankful. You didn't quite know it, but you were

a little bit lonely, when first Joy and then I deserted you. Now you've started on your own big adventure! And, Maid, I am proud that you came to tell me!"

"Oh, but we didn't! At least, that comes second!" Maidlin's innate honesty spoke out. "We came to you because we wanted something."

Jock Robertson gave his shout of laughter again. "Maid, why spoil it? Why did you tell her?"

"Oh, but I tell Ros everything!" Maidlin retorted.

"What do you want that I can do, Maid? I'm really glad there's something you want from me to-day and that you came to ask for it," Rosamund said.

"Your phone, Ros, to talk to Joy. Jock says he'll let me tell her myself, before it gets into the papers. I want it more than anything; his first present to me, Ros!"

"We shall have to wait for the call to come through. We thought we could do it in comfort here," he explained. "Will you forgive us for making use of you?"

"I'm glad you thought of it," Rosamund said heartily. "It's a beautiful idea, Maid; of course you must tell Joy yourself. Come along; we'll leave you two in possession of the phone. After that may we give you lunch?"

"We've had it, thanks. We were so hungry, with all this excitement of getting engaged," he laughed.

"And you wanted to have your first meal alone together," Rosamund's eyes laughed back at him.

" Well, afternoon tea, then. We'll have it ready for you."

" I'm going to take him to the Rose and Squirrel for tea," Maidlin began.

" Oh, good idea! Yes, that's the right place. But you can take a cup with Geoffrey and me before you go. By the way, you haven't brought any measles with you, I hope?"

Maidlin stopped short, with a wail of distress. " I forgot all about the measles! Oh, Ros, we ought not to have come!"

" Nonsense! The twinnies are still all right, aren't they?"

" Perfectly fit. They couldn't begin to show it till Monday. But I'd better not see Geoffrey-Hugh and Roddy."

" You can't carry measles about like that," Rosamund said, laughing. " Of course you forgot! What's a little thing like measles on a great day of adventure like this? Here's the phone. We'll shut you in with it; I've no doubt you can amuse yourselves while you're waiting. Do you know Joy's number, by the way?"

Maidlin stared at her. " I've never had to use it," she faltered.

" You are in love!" Rosamund mocked.

" I had a letter from Ivor three days ago," Jock said. " Don't look so worried, Maid! The number's on the letter, and I have it here. He wrote about a concert he's planning."

Maidlin gave a sigh of relief. " You think of everything. It's just as well, for I seem to be forgetting all the time."

Rosamund pushed her into the phone-room and shut the door on them both. Then she went to share the news with her husband.

CHAPTER XVII

MAIDLIN'S PERFECT DAY

" I want Lady Quellyn herself, please. It's urgent." Jock had not found it difficult to amuse Maidlin while they waited to be put through to New York.

" Who is it? Is anything the matter?" Joy's voice asked sharply.

Jock smiled and handed the instrument to Maidlin. " I give you Joy."

" Joy! Oh, Joy dear! Maid speaking. Are you really there, Joy?"

" Maid! They said it was Kentisbury. Is anything wrong?"

" No, more than all right. I had to tell you myself. Oh, Joy, Jock and I want to be married. May I, Joy? Do you mind?"

" Oh, come! You've promised," he chuckled, and spoke into the telephone. " John Robertson speaking, Lady Quellyn. Maid has promised to be my wife. Have we your good wishes?"

" Dr. Robertson!" They heard Joy's gasp of surprise.

" No—Jock!" he said promptly. " The future Mrs. Robertson will now take over."

" Joy, we're so happy. It only happened two hours ago. He asked me what I'd like to do—we

had to run away from the Abbey because of tourists
—and I said I wanted to speak to you more than
anything. So we came to Rosamund, to do it com-
fortably. It's his first present to me. Nobody
knows yet. You are pleased, aren't you, Joy? I
couldn't be quite happy if you didn't like it; but
I couldn't go back on Jock now."

"Don't you try it!" he murmured, with another
schoolboy grin.

"Maid, dear, I'm stunned. You might have
given me warning. But I am glad. He's a good
man, and he'll take care of you."

"Oh yes! He's doing that already. It's lovely
to feel so nicely looked after."

She heard Joy's laugh. "That sounds as if you'd
been neglected all your life!"

"Oh—Joy! How can you? This is different!"

"He'll attend to your music. It was his doing
you turned to oratorio, which has been your great
success and your real niche. He must understand
you very well. Yes, Maid, I am glad, and thankful.
I've felt I'd deserted you and left you lonely. Now
you're going to desert me and the twinnies."

"Not for a long time, Joy. We haven't thought
about that yet."

"What's this about a long time?" Jock protested. "May I say a word? Lady Quellyn, I'll
be very careful of her, and we'll wait till you come
home. I know she couldn't marry, or leave those
twins, unless you were at home. But you'll come
soon, won't you? I don't want to wait a long
while!"

"I congratulate you, Dr. Robertson. You've

done the wisest thing in the world. Maid's a girl worth having. See that you make her happy."

" I will. But you must make her happy too by calling me Jock. I can't be kept outside the family. Time's up, Maid. Here you are—say good-bye!"

" Good-bye, Joy, dear! I'll write a long letter to-morrow."

" You've grown up at last, Maid, and I've lost my first baby. Good luck to you, dear! Be very happy! Twinnies all right, Maid?"

" That was nice." Maidlin looked up with shining eyes. " I am so glad!"

" Now I must argue with Lord Kentisbury. He won't want me to pay for the call, but unless I do, it can't be my first present to you."

" Ros will understand that. She won't let him argue."

The discussion and the cup of tea in the Castle garden did not take long, and presently they were off again, followed by the good wishes of the Earl and Countess, to spend a long happy afternoon strolling on the turf of the Downs and ending with tea at the Rose and Squirrel, the tea-shop kept by Rosamund's young Aunt Elspeth. Jock wandered into the craft-room adjoining the tea-garden, and among the work displayed for sale he discovered a child's ring of hand-wrought silver, set with tiny blue and gold and green enamel stars which looked like daisies and forget-me-nots. It fitted Maidlin's finger and he laughed at her tiny hand as he slipped it on.

" Wear that till you can come to town and choose

the rubies I'm going to give you. You've hands
like a baby!"

" It's very pretty. I am bucked that my first
ring from you came from Rosamund's Rose Shop!
Don't give me any other one, Jock. I love this little
thing."

He laughed at her. " Rubies for you! That's
only a child's plaything. Now how do we spend
the evening?"

" You choose. I've chosen almost everything
so far."

" Quite right too. What I should really like
would be to take you home and spend a while in
your Abbey. We've rushed about the country
enough for one day."

" Oh, I'd like that! And we'll tell Anne Bellanne you're staying to dinner. The Abbey's closed
after six; we shan't have to run away again."

By her suggestion they left the car when they
reached the Abbey, and went in to wander through
the ruins. Maidlin rang up the Hall and asked for
Mary.

" Mary, dear, Jock and I are home and in the
Abbey. Presently we're coming to the house and
I want him to stay for dinner. Will that be all
right? You might warn Nan."

" We'll be delighted. Have you had a happy
day?"

" Oh, lovely! We went to tell Rosamund, and
I phoned to Joy and told her. She hadn't had my
letter about the twins and the measles; she hadn't
time even to ask for them, except just: ' Twinnies
all right?' It was obvious she didn't know; the

letter was planned to reach her on Monday. She's pleased about Jock and me, and so is Ros. Then we went on the hills and had tea at the Rose and Squirrel. A perfect day—and an hour in the Abbey will round it off beautifully. It's so odd, Mary! He always knows what I'll want to do. We like all the same things. After dinner he'll play to us, and I shall sing."

"He understands her," Mary said to herself, as she went to consult Anne. "Oh, how thankful I am! And Joy knows and approves. That's a great relief!"

Maidlin's daisy and forget-me-not ring delighted the twins, who had refused to go to bed till they had seen her.

"Can we be bridesmaids for you, like we were for Aunty Ros?" Elizabeth asked.

"I couldn't be married without you to help me, Twinnies."

"Is he going to be our really Uncle Jock?" Margaret demanded.

"I am your Uncle Jock," he said promptly.

"Well, don't men give presents to bridesmaids? Uncle Geoffrey gave us brooches."

"Margaret!" Maidlin cried. "You dreadful girl! How can you?"

"Not dreadful. Only sensible, Aunty Maid," Elizabeth said firmly. "Uncle Jock wouldn't like to give us presents we didn't want."

"And you don't want brooches again. I quite agree, Miss Twin, whichever you are. We'd better know what you'd like to have." Jock's lips were twitching in amusement.

" Don't you know us which is which?" Margaret leaned on his knee and gazed up at him.

" Are you the one who was in the tree? Or are you the one who came running for help?"

" I was the kitten in the beashly tree; I'm Margaret Joan Marchwood."

" And I'm Elizabeth Joy Marchwood; I'm older than her. You didn't think our name was Quellyn, did you?" Elizabeth took possession of his other knee.

" No, I quite understand that you are Marchwood twins. I knew your father very well."

The twins gazed at him with round brown eyes. Their father had always seemed like a person in a fairy-tale.

" What was he like?" Elizabeth burst out.

" A big man who liked adventures."

" We like adventures too."

" I know you do. Now what about those presents for my bridesmaids? What would you like them to be?"

But Elizabeth turned suddenly and most unusually shy and hung her head. " Aunty Maid said Twin was a dreadful girl. Let the presents be anything you like, Uncle Jock."

" Will we be your bridesmaids?" Margaret asked. " I thought we'd be hers."

" But I'm going to be married too, so I want bridesmaids as well, don't I? Won't you help me to choose the presents? You tell me, Margaret."

" Watches, to wear on our arms!" Margaret shouted. " Like all real ladies have!"

Dr. Jock threw back his head and laughed. " A

very good choice! Wrist-watches it shall be. Maid, you'd better make your plans and name the day. We mustn't keep those watches waiting too long for their new mothers."

Elizabeth chuckled. "You are funny! I do like you!"

" Margaret will break a wrist-watch in half an hour," Maidlin said. " She's a very careless girl."

" I won't! I'm not! Aunty Maid, I never will!" Margaret stormed. " I'm not as bad as that!"

" Now you know which is Margaret," Maidlin remarked. " The noisy one; you'll remember her!"

" The shrieker," said Lindy, coming to fetch the children. " Twins, it's long past time for bed. Come along to Nelly!"

CHAPTER XVIII

TELLING JOY

" MARGARET'S mouth hurts her. I suppose she means her throat's sore," Lindy reported to Mary on Monday evening. " And Elizabeth looks as if she'd been crying, but she hasn't. She says she has a headache."

" Then we aren't going to escape," Mary said heavily. " Thanks, Lindy. Will you ask Maidlin and Nan to come to my room? I'll ring up the doctor."

In her study she told the news to the other two.

" Oh, Mary!" Maidlin looked at her in horror, her radiant happiness suddenly dimmed. " I'd forgotten all about the measles! Mary, isn't life *mixed*? I've been so wildly joyful this week-end!"

" It's made us all happy just to see you, and it has helped us to forget, too," Mary said. " Maid, dear, life is mixed, and it will go on being mixed. And it wouldn't be worth much if it were not mixed, Maid."

" No, I suppose not," Maidlin admitted. " We need to face up to both things. But this is a real blow. If only they could have escaped!"

" Well, at least they'll have it together and we shall get it over," Anne said practically. " I've been in terror that Margaret would start—it would be Margaret first, of course!—and that we'd have to separate them; and then in a fortnight Elizabeth would begin, and it would hang about for weeks. They'll be company for one another."

"Dr Brown is coming at once, and he's sending in a good nurse, and we can have a second if we need her. Now we must plan things in the best way for ourselves," Mary began.

"There's nothing to plan. It's all decided," Lindy said instantly. "I'm going to stay in the room with them; I'm the assistant nurse. Nan will see to everybody's meals. Mary will look after the house, and Miss Maid will sing to us downstairs."

"Not likely! I'm not going to be left out," Maidlin exclaimed.

Mary took charge of the situation and spoke in a tone of authority she rarely used. "Maid, dear, you're the difficulty. Don't make things harder for us all! We know you want to be with the children, but you aren't needed and it just isn't possible for you. You don't belong only to yourself now; you have Dr. Jock to think of. You've been engaged to him for three days; you couldn't ask him to do without you for a fortnight."

Maidlin sat looking down at the beautiful ruby ring she had chosen in town that morning, which she wore beside the silver circlet of daisies and forget-me-nots. "You mean, I must keep away from the twins for the whole time they are ill?"

"You can't keep running in and out. Dr. Jock would never forgive us if you ran the risk of infection. As you came home so late, you haven't seen the children since this morning, when they seemed perfectly fit and well. I don't suppose there's any risk to you, if you keep away from them now."

" But I want to be with them!" Maidlin cried. " If Joy were here it would be different. I ought to take her place, Mary!"

" Joy wouldn't ask it of you now. Maid, you'll have to sacrifice your own feelings. I know it's hard; but you'll make things worse for all of us unless you give in."

" At least, wait and see how things go!" Anne urged. " If the children were very ill you might feel you must be with them, but it's not at all likely. They're in very good health; we've seen to that during this last fortnight. They'll probably have it quite lightly."

" But they'll be so frightened!" Maidlin wailed. " They've never had anything; they won't understand. When the rash comes out——"

" We shall play at being spotty pigs," Lindy said promptly. " I shall have a competition to see who has most spots, and a prize. We'll turn it into a game."

" Oh, Miss Belinda, what a treasure you are!" Maidlin laughed and half cried at the same time. " But couldn't you make it spotted dogs? It sounds so much better!"

" The nurse will know how to talk to them, if she's any good at all," Mary added. " Maid, you're needed outside the hospital ward. There must be someone to see visitors and answer inquiries; that's your job. And first, what are you going to do about telling Joy?"

They looked at one another, and then all looked at Maidlin. This was definitely her department.

" We must cable at once. Joy will have to know. I hope my letter has arrived." Maidlin's lips pinched. " She'll have a horrible shock, if she hasn't had it. I need only say: ' Sorry. Twins measles.' I told her what plans we had made and promised to have the best possible nurse. She knows we'll do all we can."

" There's the phone," Mary said. " Shall I go? It's sure to be for you."

" I'll go. But it can't be Jock, unless he's rung up on his way back to town." In spite of her distress Maidlin's eyes laughed at Mary, for this had happened twice already, when Jock, after bringing her home, had called her up from some village on his road to say last forgotten words: " Maid, I just want to ask you——" " Maid, I meant to tell you——"

In a few moments Maidlin returned to the conference. " It was a cable from Joy; she's had the letter. She says: ' Please cable news of children.' I'm glad; it makes it easier for her. I sent the cable at once, by phone; I said almost what we'd planned: ' Sorry. Fear twins measles.' The doctor hasn't confirmed it yet; I hope after he's been I'll be able to send another message: ' Doing well. Slight attack.' But that can't be till to-morrow."

" And you used to be terrified of the phone!" Mary remarked.

" I was silly. It was when Rosamund left us to go to Switzerland that I had to get over that particular fright of mine. I was so keen to speak to her that I forgot to be nervous. Lindy Bellanne, you're quite sure you're willing to be the one to stay in quarantine for a fortnight?" Maidlin asked anxiously. " It seems awfully mean to let you do it."

" I want to do it," Lindy insisted. " I haven't any outside engagements, your sort or any other kind. I shall love to nurse the kids."

" It's the most tremendous help to us," Maidlin said wistfully. " You know how much I want to be with them myself."

The doctor refused to give any opinion on the seriousness or otherwise of the twins' condition till the morning. Next day the children were feverish, Margaret especially so, and were both feeling too ill to be interested in Lindy's game of spotted dog. Elizabeth cheered up during the afternoon and was much intrigued by her own appearance and amused at Margaret's hot flushed face; but Margaret could not be brought to realise that she had won the competition and that a prize for spots awaited her. Her temperature went up and up, and she began to talk wildly and then to shout. The nurse carried Elizabeth into the next room, in spite of her wails of protest, and left her in Lindy's charge, while she watched by Margaret. The doctor came again, looked at Margaret, and phoned for a night nurse.

" That child ought never to be allowed to have a temperature," he said irritably. " I know you weren't to blame. But she's highly strung, and it's not two years since she had that bad time of concussion, when she fell into the well in the crypt. This is going to take a lot out of her. You'd better let her mother know; she can't do anything, but we daren't keep it from her. You'll cable at once, Madalena; say: ' Elizabeth doing well. Margaret bad attack.' I'm sorry for Lady Quellyn, but there's no help for it.''

Maidlin, white and anxious, sent the cable and then rang up Dr. Jock.

'' Jock, Margaret's really bad. Her temp.'s very high. I can't bear it, Jock. I must be with her. I promised to tell you before I went to her.''

There was a moment's pause. When his answer came there was a note in Jock's voice she had never yet heard.

'' I can't ask you not to go. I know what it means to you. But—oh, Maid, my dearest, be careful, for my sake! You told me you had the thing very badly as a child. If anything happened to you now—if you were ill and in danger—I couldn't bear it, Maid.''

The pause before answering was Maidlin's this time. At last she spoke. '' Jock, I didn't know how much you cared. I hadn't quite understood. Jock, I'll wait till the morning, for your sake, if I possibly can. I'll tell Nurse only to send for me if Margaret's really in danger. It hasn't come to that yet; perhaps they'll bring her temp. down. I don't want you to be thinking about us all night—and you have that Queen's Hall concert. Jock, I promise faithfully I won't go near the children unless it's absolutely necessary; there's a second nurse coming. But you know I couldn't stay away if— if Margaret——''

'' God bless you, dear. Thank you for that promise. I know what a sacrifice it means. For my sake, take care of yourself, Maid."

" I will; really I will, Jock, dear." Maidlin rang off, and then dropped into the nearest chair. " But it means a bad night for Mary and me. It wouldn't be so hard if we could do anything to help."

The phone rang, and she picked up the receiver. " Is it Jock again?"

Then she stiffened into rigid attention at the tidings: " New York wants you. Please hold on."

" Joy! She hasn't waited for to-day's news. I shall have to tell her."

At last Joy's voice came. " Is that Maidlin?"

" Yes, Joy, dear. I've just cabled you. Elizabeth's all right, lots of spots, but getting on well; her temp. has come down, and the doctor says it's a slight attack. Her only trouble is that we've had to separate them. Margaret's rather bad, I'm afraid. Her temp.'s very high, so Nurse sent Elizabeth to another room."

" Is Margaret in danger?" Joy asked sharply.

" The doctor didn't say that, but he's talking about her illness two years ago, and he says she's highly strung. I'll cable again, as soon as there's any change." With a great effort Maidlin kept her voice steady.

" Well, Maid, listen carefully. I'm coming home, as soon as Ivor can find me a berth on a quick boat. I must see the children for myself. I'm not bringing David; he's had bottles for a month now, so he doesn't need me; Nurse is splendid, and Ivor will be here to get her more help if necessary. I'll cable you the name of the boat and the date I sail, and I hope I'll be with you quite soon. But—this is urgent, Maid! I must have news during the voyage, or I shall go crazy. You must radio the ship each day; Dr. Robertson will find out how to do it and send the messages for you. Let me have the latest news, Maid; get him to help you."

" Oh, Joy!" Maidlin was almost in tears of relief. " Can you really come? Joy, we want you so badly!"

" If the children are better I can only stay for a week or two. Ivor and I have engagements next month; he really needs me. But after a time like this, I must see for myself that they're all right. Maid, have you been with them?"

" Nobody will let me go to them." Maidlin caught her breath in a sob. " Joy, I want to go so much, but everybody keeps me away. And Jock——"

" You mustn't go into infection. You were terribly ill when you had it before. Don't go near them, Maid. The nurses will do everything. Dr. Jock would never forgive us if you were ill. And I'm sure he comes to see you every day. You mustn't be in quarantine."

" That's what everybody says. But I've told him that I shall go if Margaret's really in danger, Joy."

" You couldn't do any more than the nurses will do. Take care of yourself, dear! I'm so sorry." And then time was up.

Maidlin rang Jock again, to give this news and

to beg for his help. Then she went racing up to Mary's room.

"Mary! Oh, Mary, Joy's coming—as soon as ever she can—just for a week or two! Won't it be wonderful to have her here? We must tell Elizabeth. It will cheer her up more than anything!"

CHAPTER XIX

DR. JOCK MAKES PLANS

IT was a bad night for everybody—except, indeed, for Elizabeth, who slept peacefully, watched by Lindy. Margaret tossed, and talked, and cried out for "Twin" and her mother, and the nurse looked grave, but refused to send for Maidlin.

"Not yet," she said, time after time.

Maidlin and Mary sat together in Mary's room, waiting in dread of a summons. There was no need for words; each knew everything that the other was thinking. Maidlin crouched on a stool by the fire, and Mary put her arm round her and held her tightly.

After his concert Jock rang up to ask for news and to say what he could in the way of comfort. He had made inquiries as to radio cables and would send on every message Maidlin wished. The talk cheered her for a moment, but fear came back, and she went to the shelter of Mary's arms again.

"I wish he could have been here with us," she whispered.

"He'll come in the morning, dear!"

" I'm afraid of the morning, Mary. What if Margaret has a collapse, after this high fever? Doesn't that happen in the morning?"

" Perhaps it won't. We want her temp. to come down."

" I'm frightened," Maidlin said brokenly, and set herself to endure the night's agony of suspense as bravely as she could.

The morning brought hope. Margaret was better, and, though very limp and weak, seemed more herself. She was puzzled to find no twin beside her and wept wearily, but fell into a healing sleep which lasted all day, to the delight of doctor and nurses.

Lindy invented endless new games and stories to keep Elizabeth contented, but most effective of all was the promise that she should see her mother soon, if only she was a good girl and let Twin have a long sleep. Maidlin, very grateful for Lindy, sent a cheerful cable to Joy and rang up Jock, asking him not to come till the afternoon. Then she and Mary went to bed and slept till lunch-time.

When Jock appeared Maidlin was ready to go out with him, for Margaret was still asleep and all seemed likely to be well. They left the car and climbed the hill behind the Hall, and she showed him the strange straight path leading to the Abbey, cutting across roads and through the woods, and led him to the monk's cell in the quarry from which it started.

" I've come to ask an urgent question," he said, as they sat on the edge of the hollow in the healing wind and gazed down at the Abbey and out to Thame and Oxford.

Maidlin looked up from the picnic basket he had brought, which she was exploring, and a smile danced in her dark eyes. " But I thought you had asked me? Is anything else really important?"

" No," he laughed, delighting in the return of her true self after the distress of the night. " Nothing else really matters, now that the big thing is settled."

" What is it going to be like, being married to you?"

The smile was in Jock's eyes this time. " The nicest thing in the world."

" Oh, of course! I've been so happy at the Abbey, with Joy and the children and all our crowd, that it will have to be most terribly nice to make up for leaving home. I'm willing to risk it." Maidlin flung her laughing look at him. " But I want to know what to expect. I suppose it will mean living in London. I've always loved the country, but there's your work."

" And yours," he said. " But why? If Ivor can live at the Hall, and if you can live there and go home after singing in town, why can't I?"

" Oh!" Her face lit up. " Could we live in the country, Jock?"

" I haven't any house for you—yet. We shall have to find one. I don't see why it shouldn't be in the country; we have the car. Not too far out, of course, but certainly not in town. We'll find the place and then we'll build our house. It will be jolly to plan it as we wish."

" That would be fun. I've had lovely homes,
but they've always been other people's. Kentisbury is almost like a home to me now."

" I can't build you anything the size of Kentisbury!" He sat up in pretended dismay. " Are
you expecting it? We'll rent Windsor Castle."

" Silly!" Her laugh rang out. " I want a little
house."

" Your laugh has all your singing voice in it.
I love to make you laugh. You can't have a little
house—not for our home. You must have something worthy of you. We'll build our house—a
nice one—and we'll call it—I wonder!"

" Not the Hall, or the Manor, or the Grange,
or the Castle, or the Park! We have all those in
the family already," Maidlin warned him, as she
spread out the tea things.

" We'll put the house in Sussex. Then we can
call it The Pallant."

" The Pallant?" Maidlin stared at him. " What
an odd word! What does it mean?"

" I've no idea, but I've seen houses in Sussex
called The Pallant."

Maidlin's rich laugh rang out again. " Silly!
It's a jolly name. I'd love to live at The Pallant.
But you must find out what it means. It might be
something horrible, like a pigsty."

" No, it's something dignified and ecclesiastical.
There's a Pallant in Chichester, whatever it is, near
the Cathedral. I wouldn't ask you to live in a
pigsty. Our house will be gracious and beautiful
and you'll be the perfect hostess, and we'll invite

great musicians to dinner and struggling ones for week-ends.''

'' I like that idea!'' Maidlin exclaimed. '' The great people for dinner-parties—yes; but the beginners for week-ends in the country. How lovely, Jock!''

'' Aren't you the least curious about my urgent question? I must have an answer to-day.''

'' I didn't know you really meant it. Oh, do tell me! I want to know badly.''

'' A friend of mine is down on his luck. He has a job offered him abroad, and he wants to get his house off his hands. He'd like to sell quickly; he needs the cash for his expenses in starting. It's near the Sussex coast, in a little town, and it's a tiny place. I've seen it; a bungalow, with three small rooms and one still smaller, a nice bit of garden, no garage, a good kitchen and bathroom. He wants a thousand for it, and if he could have it quickly it would make all the difference to him. Now that we've settled about our real home—The Pallant, you know—the point is this: would you like me to buy the little house near the sea, to be a sort of country cottage that we could run away to and have all to ourselves when we wanted to escape?''

Maidlin looked at him, her face ablaze. '' Jock! Would you? A hidie-hole, just for you and me, where I could be the cook and you'd be the gardener and do the odd jobs?''

Jock threw back his head and laughed. '' Exactly what was in my mind! There's no room for the littlest maid, and I'd have to park the car somewhere and trudge half a mile to fetch her. We'd have to do everything for ourselves.''

'' We'd play at it,'' Maidlin cried with enthusiasm. '' A doll's house to play with! Oh, Jock, buy it! Don't lose it! I'd love to play with it!''

'' It's not a cottage. It has gas and electric light, and it's well built, and in many ways it's very attractive. We could always sell it again, but perhaps until The Pallant is ready——'' he began.

Maidlin rocked with happy laughter. '' You must find out what that funny word means before you talk as if it was settled! Jock, I said I wanted a little house, but I know it isn't possible; you must have a proper place, to ask your friends to dinner in, and I must take care of it for you. But I'd simply love a baby house to play with!''

'' It's not much more than a but and a ben. You know about cottages in the Highlands being just two rooms, the but, or the outer one, and the ben, the inner room? That's what the little house is like. We could put it on the gate—The But and Ben.''

'' People would think we were mad.''

'' To be in the fashion, we ought to call it ' Dunroamin',' or ' Justit,' or ' Youandi.' I've seen all those lately,'' he began.

'' I won't! I won't live with you in ' Youandi '!''

'' Well, still more fashionable would be ' Maijo ' —Maid and Jock, you know. Or ' Jocmay.' That's the very latest idea in the neighbourhood.''

'' We won't be in the fashion, then.''

'' Would you like to see the little house?''

'' Oh, I would! When can we go?''

" As soon as I've a whole day free. I'll ring you up and let you know. Quite soon; I must decide at once. Good thing you listened to me last night! Aren't you glad you aren't in quarantine for a fortnight?"

Maidlin clasped her hands round her knees and gazed at him. " Yes, I am—now. But we felt fearful last night."

" I know. I heard it in your voice. It's over; young Margaret is through the worst, and the nurses will do all that she needs. I want you to forget last night. We can't have tragedy just now. That's why I told you about the little house."

" We might call it that—The Little House," Maidlin said dreamily. " I love the thought of it. I've always wanted a cottage to play in."

" The day we're married I shall make the house yours," he said. " Then when we have dreadful quarrels, and you find out what a fearful temper I have, and what a very ordinary sort of chap I am, you can say, ' I'm going away to my own house,' and order out the car and shove off, leaving me, crushed and lonely, at The Pallant."

Maidlin rocked with laughter again. " Every time you say that funny name I have to laugh! I'd love to feel the little house was mine, but I shan't need to run away from you. I'm the one with the temper—you don't know! I'm dreadful. You'll turn me out of the—The Pallant!—and say: ' Go to your own house, woman, and don't come back to me till you're in your right mind!' It will be very convenient to have two houses! But I'm sorry about there being no garage," she added.

" It's hard luck on you. Do you mind? Where will you keep the car?"

" There's a good place round the corner, on the London road, which by-passes an ancient village. It will be good for me; keep me from getting fat! I'll go round for the car while you're powdering your nose. We'll go to see the little house as soon as ever we can," he promised.

CHAPTER XX

PRIZES FOR TWINS

" WHAT'S the prize for spots, Aunty Lin?" Margaret asked languidly. " I had most; Nurse said so. I've won."

" But that isn't fair!" Elizabeth protested as, restored to her twin's side, she sat up in the same bed and stared at Lindy. " She did have lots of spots, so she has won; but she was a horrid nuisance to everybody. I heard Nurse say Twin gave you all a lot of bother. I ought to have a prize because I was the gooder one. It's easy to have spots; you can't help it, they just come; but it isn't ever easy to be good. You said I was good, Aunt Belinda!"

" There's something in that." Lindy, in a big white apron and a cap borrowed from Nurse, was playing at hospitals. " It sounds to me as if you'd both need to have prizes. Won't it be prize enough to have your mother quite soon?"

" Want prizes now." Margaret, still very weak, showed signs of tears.

Elizabeth regarded her sternly. "Now don't you begin again, Twin! You never cried so much before. I shall tell Andy, and he'll laugh."

Margaret swallowed a sob. "He won't. And you're not to tell. It would be—it would be caddish to tell about a girl who's ill."

"Yes, it would," Lindy said severely. "Elizabeth won't do anything so caddish; don't worry! What do you want for prizes?"

"Forget-me-nots and daisies, like Aunty Maid's." Margaret forgot to weep and spoke eagerly. "New Uncle Jock said they was meant for girls, not ladies. Has the shop got any more?"

"Rings, do you mean? You never wear rings," Lindy protested.

"Because we haven't got any to wear," Elizabeth pointed out.

"You'd lose them in a week."

"We wouldn't! We wouldn't!" Margaret began to jump about her bed.

Lindy, inwardly rejoicing to see the old Margaret coming back, was outwardly stern and scolded her into lying down again. "You don't want to be ill when your mother comes."

"Mother would get a fright, if she saw you look like I saw you," Elizabeth remarked. "You were as red as fire, and as for spots—you was all over them, Twin."

"They were all over her, you mean," Lindy observed.

"I wasn't! I didn't! Twin, it's caddish of you to remember," Margaret wailed.

"I couldn't ever forget. You did look funny!

But Nurse came and whisked me away," Elizabeth said seriously, " so I don't know what you looked like in the night. Awful, I should think!"

" Elizabeth, you're being unkind," Lindy said sharply. " Margaret was very clever to have such a nice rash. If it hadn't come out she'd have been much more ill. You're not to tease her. If you do there won't be any prize for you. You won't like it if Twin has a daisy ring and you have none."

This horrible idea sobered Elizabeth completely. " I'll be as good as I've ever been in my life," she promised hurriedly. " I'll be as good as the angels in the church windows."

" We shan't believe it's you, if you are," Margaret said instantly.

Lindy stifled a laugh. " I'll call out of the window to Aunty Maid and ask about the rings, but you won't have them till you're better, and only if you've been really good girls," she warned them.

" If I have a daisy ring and Elizabeth-Twin doesn't, people will always know us which is which," Margaret remarked. " Jolly good plan, I think!"

" If you have one and I don't, I—I shall take yours and stamp on it!" Elizabeth cried heatedly.

" Then you'd better begin practisin' being a church-window angel," Margaret retorted with much satisfaction.

Lindy leaned out of her window that evening and called down to Maidlin on the terrace, telling of the twins' request. " I don't know what to do. They've set their hearts on daisy rings. I meant to buy the prizes; I knew there would have to be two, of course! They'd have thought of some excuse. Are the rings very expensive?"

"Very cheap. Jock and I will see to that for you," Maidlin called back to her. "We're going to have a long day out to-morrow; we want to run down to the sea. I'll ask him to go past the Rose and Squirrel and we'll see if they have any more rings. You'd better measure the exact size with bits of string."

"That will intrigue my patients. I'll see to it. Thanks so much! What was that you were singing just now?"

"*In a Persian Garden* again. Jock wants me to sing it for him at Queen's Hall in June."

"We loved it. We heard quite well."

"Aren't you getting very tired of being up there? You don't know how grateful we are. Nurse says the way you manage the children is marvellous."

"I go for a walk every day while they're asleep. Mostly I dash into the orchard, but sometimes I go to the Manor lake, where I first saw the kiddies, as the family's still away. Are you getting piles of congratulations and letters?"

"Oh, heaps!" Maidlin laughed. "It would have been much more peaceful to be in quarantine!"

"Dr. Jock wouldn't have liked it. I'm glad I was here."

"I'm glad, too, and Joy will be very much obliged to you."

"I want to see her. Is she really like the twins?

I asked them what she was like, and they both said together: ' Just like us.' Is she?"

" She is." Maidlin smiled. " Give the twinnies my love and tell them I'll find out about the prizes to-morrow."

" They're not to have them till they're better. It's the only way I can keep Elizabeth in order," Lindy explained. " She's so much better than Margaret that she's ready to tease and be a nuisance, but she becomes angelic in a moment if I point out that Twin will have a daisy ring and she won't."

" You know how to manage her. I expect you were a good prefect at school! You'd better give up the idea of singing and be trained as a children's nurse, Skylark!" Maidlin smiled up at the window.

" The twins want to know—if I'm a skylark, what is Aunty Maid? I said, the blackbird, of course! So now they listen every evening for Aunty Maid up in a tree. I won't give up unless you think I won't be any good at singing."

" I know you'll be very good. Jock says so too. We're going to help young musicians of every kind; you'd better be our first protégée. We'll see you through your training! I'm in earnest, Belinda Bellanne; it isn't a joke." And Maidlin went indoors, leaving Lindy radiant.

The Rose Shop was able to provide two very small daisy rings, and Maidlin put them into her bag thankfully, for they represented the bait which was to keep the twins in order during their convalescence. Then she rejoined Jock in the car and they sped away to the sea to find the little house.

" Jock, you won't ever let them make you a baronet, as they did Ivor, will you?" Maidlin asked. " I don't want to be ' My Lady '! I'd much rather be Mrs. Robertson."

" I haven't heard any suggestion of it," he assured her.

" They often do it to music people. Of course, you ought to have it, just as much as Ivor," Maidlin admitted.

He laughed. " I thought you felt I hadn't deserved it."

" Don't be silly! You deserve it more than anybody. But so many of us are called ' My Lady.' I don't want to be another. Mrs. Robertson's much nicer."

" If a knighthood or a baronetcy is offered me, I'll say my wife doesn't wish me to accept."

" Oh! I don't know——" Maidlin began.

Jock laughed again. " The question isn't pressing. Nobody has asked me if I'd like to be Sir John. Have you found a name for your house yet?"

" I want to see it first. What is it called now?"

" Sunnyside," he said gravely. " There seems to be a Sunnyside in every street in the town. I really couldn't bear Sunnyside. In any case, I should have called it Shadyside; the house looks north."

" Oh! Isn't that cold?"

" Wait and see," he advised.

" If it's so small there won't be room for a piano. We shall have to do without music."

" Not while you're there. And I'm quite a useful bass. We'll find a tenor and invite your little soprano and have unaccompanied quartets, as they did in Elizabethan days. And there will be room for Violetta. You'll let me bring Violetta the Viola, I hope?"

Maidlin turned startled eyes on him. " A viola? But how marvellous! I didn't know!"

" I was first viola in an orchestra for three years. You should have known I'd played orchestrally; the only question should have been: ' What was your instrument?' "

" I didn't think," she apologised. " Of course, you would play something besides the piano. A viola! I'll love that. The deep notes are so beautiful."

" The contralto of the strings," he agreed. " Like your voice—high notes and low; fiddle voice and 'cello voice all in one. Violetta has a lovely tone. I hope you'll like the lady. She's the only girl I ever cared about till I met you."

" I shall love Violetta, and she'll be just right for the little house." Maidlin smiled at him.

" I believe you mean to call it that. Or The Small House, like in Trollope's novel."

" Is it in a street? It would seem funny to live in a street after the Hall and the farm on the fells."

" It is in a street, but it's a wide street, with trees. If I had to leave you there and run up to town, you'd have the advantage of having neighbours without the disadvantage of feeling overlooked."

" Everything perfect, in fact! You sound as if you'd planned it just for us." Maidlin laughed.

CHAPTER XXI

MAIDLIN'S LITTLE HOUSE

Jock drew up the car and waved his hand. "Madam, your little house. Your bungalow, in fact."

Eager-eyed, Maidlin gazed at a long low house between two large ones set in big gardens. It had rough-cast grey walls, lattice windows in dark-brown frames, and a dark-red roof sweeping down and broken by one dormer window.

"Oh, pretty!" she exclaimed. "Wait a moment before we go in! I want to make friends with it. It looks as if it's waiting for us. But it looks shy, as if it ought not to be here among the bigger houses."

"Modest," Jock said. "Like us."

Maidlin gave a low laugh. "Modest! You boss great orchestras, and I sing in the Albert Hall to ten thousand people! Is modest quite the right word for you and me?"

"Ten million people. Don't forget your radio audience. All the same, we're both shy and retiring, and your little house looks as if it might just suit us."

Maidlin opened the door of the car and sprang out, and stood looking up at the house. It had a wooden fence and a small gate, and the little garden was gay with blue and white hyacinths and a big bush of flaring orange berberis.

" Take care!" Jock called, as she opened the gate.

He was too late, and she gasped in surprise as she took a much longer step down to the path than she had expected.

" That isn't very safe. We'll have to raise that path, or warn people. Jock!" she cried, whirling round. " The name for the little house—Step Down! Oh, do let's call it Step Down! I never heard of a house called Step Down before!"

" Meaning that it's a step down to marry me?"

" Silly! Nobody could fall down if they'd read that name on the gate!"

He laughed. " The locals will think you can't spell. One of the hills behind the town is Steep Down; they'll think that's what you mean."

" Not when they've fallen into our path, as I did. They'll say: ' What a clever name!' Now open the door and show me the inside of Step Down!"

He laughed again. Her excitement over the house was giving him keen joy and amusement.

" A glass door with a coloured pattern; that's pretty," Maidlin exclaimed.

" Two glass doors with coloured patterns," he amended.

He opened the first, to show a tiny hall, six feet long and only four feet wide, with a cupboard of dark-brown wood for coats and umbrellas, and with walls papered a soft yellow. A second glass door closed the hall; he opened this and waved her forward.

" Madam, the whole of your little house lies before you."

M

Maidlin darted to his side. " Oh, Jock! Is that all of it? It *is* a dolls' house! Oh, how simply perfect!"

A narrow passage, with yellow walls, ran across the house, at right angles to the hall. Three brown doors faced them, standing open. Maidlin ran to the nearest and found herself in a sitting-room, where a square bay window looked into the garden, with two red-brick steps leading down from a glass door.

" Show me the whole house, Jock! I'll look at each room carefully afterwards. What are the other rooms?"

" What we like to make them. But I suggest this small one should be my dressing-room, and this much nicer one should be the bedroom."

" Three rooms, all in a line and all looking into the garden. How clever!" Maidlin commented. " And across the passage? Oh, the kitchen and bathroom; what a jolly kitchen! Look at the cupboards!"

" I was rather struck with the kitchen myself," he agreed.

Maidlin ran about making discoveries. " That's the larder; quite a decent scullery and sink, and a door to shut it off from the kitchen—oh, good! Here's the back door, so the milk and bread don't need to come in by the glass door. Oh, look at the coal-hole! And a gas-stove, and an Ideal boiler; it's awfully well fitted up, Jock. Do you know what I feel like?"

" A little girl who has been given a new dolls' house."

" Just what I was going to say! How did you know?"

" It's written all over you. You've lived so long in Halls and Castles and Manors that you've fallen completely in love with a hovel."

" Oh, it's not! It's a dear little place! What a decent bathroom! And here's another wee room, looking to the front. What is this for?"

" A glory-hole, to keep everything in—especially music and books. We could put in an extra bed, in case you want to keep Miss Belinda for a night, and a table, where we could work. There's a big useful cupboard. But *I* think this little room is where you'll retreat to in the summer, when it will be beautifully cool and shady. Those other rooms face south."

" They'll have sun pouring in all day; lovely! It *is* well planned, Jock! The kitchen is cool, but our rooms will be gloriously sunny."

" Blazing hot, till evening, in the summer," he teased. " But you can retreat to the kitchen or this north room; they'll seem quite chilly in comparison. Now that's the whole of it, except the loft. I haven't seen the loft yet, but it looks extremely useful. I'm going to hunt for a ladder."

Maidlin, inexperienced in household management, did not realise the importance of the loft for storage space in such a very small dwelling. She continued her explorations, and found a cupboard for brooms or carpet-sweeper, and then went into the big bedroom, pushed open a lattice-window, and leaned on the wide ledge to survey the garden.

A good-sized lawn, roses trained up posts, a wide

patch for flowers and currant bushes, two apple
trees, a beautiful pink japonica covered with bloom,
a small shed from which came Jock's cheerful
whistle as he wrestled with the ladder; that was the
whole of it, but it had high wooden fences and it
felt very private.

" Just big enough for two people to take care of,
and a little of everything in it.   It's very well
thought out," Maidlin murmured contentedly, and
then she forgot the garden and went off into a happy
dream, marvelling, as she had been doing for all
the last week, at this wonderful new sense of com-
panionship which had come to her and had satisfied
her so entirely. Always, even with Joy, she had
kept a secret reserve; it had been unconscious but
inevitable, because Joy had not quite understood
her in spite of her love, and once at least had failed
her badly. Maidlin's love in return had been un-
changed, but her unconscious self had not forgotten. Now she felt something new; her trust in
Jock's understanding was absolute and to him all
her reserves were down. She seemed to herself a
new person; and she looked it, lit by an inner con-
fidence and content which radiated from her all the
time.

" Jock!" She turned from the window as she
heard his step. " Do you see the concrete path
under the windows? We'll have breakfast out there
in the sun, while the lawn's still dripping with dew,
and we'll tame the robins and chaffinches to come
on to the table; they'll soon learn. It's a dear little
garden, Jock, and I do love the wide brown window-
sills."

"Can't live on window-sills," he grinned. "Coming up to see the loft?"

"I shall keep bowls of bulbs and jars of flowers on them. I can see it all as it will look when it's furnished. It's a Camp Fire house already; yellow walls and brown wood. We'll keep it like this, and have brown curtains and carpets and golden cushions, and brown and gold pottery like Mary-Dorothy's."

"What's Camp Fire?" he asked, placing the ladder in position.

"A part of me you don't know about yet, just as I didn't know about your viola. I'll show you my gown and tell you all about it. Are we going up there?"

"I am. Don't come, if you're frightened."

"I'm not a scrap frightened. You go first and haul me up; I must see the whole of our house."

"Now what do you really feel about it?" he asked, as they stood by the loft window and discovered a glimpse of green hills between the houses opposite. "It has no outlook except the garden, and there isn't really room for even a little maid. You can almost stand in the middle and touch the whole of it. Is it too pokey?"

"It's lovely, and I don't want a maid. I want to play at house and be the cook. Please buy it, Jock! I couldn't bear to lose Step Down now!"

"It shall be your wedding-gift. On the day you marry me Step Down will be yours."

"Would next week be too soon?" Maidlin's eyes gleamed in a rare touch of mischief.

"To-morrow, if you like," he said promptly.

" No, I must have time to enjoy being engaged. And I have to get ready. But buy the little house, Jock! I want it for our own."

" Shall we have our honeymoon in it? No, I think not. I can't let you cook and wash up on your honeymoon."

Maidlin turned a radiant face to him. " I meant to tell you, but this dear little place made me forget. Rosamund talked to me on the phone last night, and she wants to lend us their place in Scotland— Vairy Castle. It's quite small, but big enough for two, and there's a kind housekeeper who would look after us. Ros and Geoffrey went there a year ago and loved it. The castle is close to a loch and there are boats. Don't you like the sound of it?"

" Sounds exactly right. Tell the Countess we accept, with hearty thanks."

" I'll love to see Scotland. We'll go by car, and we'll stop in Cumberland to show you the little old farm where I lived till I was fourteen. I was a horribly difficult, awkward child."

" No music, I suppose?"

" None at all. I didn't know I wanted it. Joy discovered that and told me I had a voice that could be trained."

" My blessings on Lady Joy!" Jock said with heartfelt gratitude, as he helped her carefully on to the ladder again. " No wonder you were awkward and miserable! Quite half of you was being smothered."

" But the other half learned a lot about cooking, and keeping a house clean," Maidlin assured him. " I haven't had to use all that part of me for years, but it's there. The aunts trained me in house-keeping. I shall love to housekeep for you."

"With me," he corrected. "I shall help. I shall wipe the dishes and clean the knives and shoes."

Maidlin's laugh rang out. "What would the orchestra say? Their beloved Doc-Jock turned boot-boy! A real step down!"

"They'd be annoyed with me for letting you do kitchen-work."

"We won't tell the orchestra. We'll talk about our house at the seaside, and they'll think we keep a large staff of servants."

"And they'll wonder why nobody is invited to the seaside residence. We must find the right spot and begin to build The Pallant."

Maidlin's eyes danced. "The Pallant and Step Down! We are funny people, aren't we?"

"I'm much funnier than you are," Jock boasted. "At least you know what Step Down means!"

"You'd better find out what The Pallant means," Maidlin laughed. "I won't live in it unless I know. Dear little Step Down! We're going to take care of you now."

"And if we get tired of you we can always sell you again," Jock added.

"Or lend it to people. That would be much jollier. It would be a lovely place for two people for a holiday, if we don't want to use it ourselves."

"Step Down, you'll be kept busy. You're going to have lots of fun," said Jock.

CHAPTER XXII

JOY COMES HOME

" HAVE you solved your problem, Anne Bell-anne?" Maidlin asked, when she had told Mary and Anne about Step Down.

" How marvellous of you to remember, in all the thrills of your engagement!" Anne exclaimed. " I'd been wondering if I might speak to you. I've enjoyed being cook-in-charge, and organising my kitchen and the work and meals, far more than I expected, but that's partly because I've had my first experience of it in this beautiful place. Will Lady Quellyn let Mrs. Spindle come back? Or do you think I could possibly satisfy her? Would she let me try?"

" I'm sure she would, but about Susan Spindle, of course I can't say. She's a very old friend of the house, and Joy has a baby boy herself and will know how much Susan wanted to see her baby. Perhaps she'll forgive her and take her back, as the twins are better. If she does, would you con-sider the idea of helping me?" Maidlin asked eagerly. " I'd like so much to have you."

Anne's face lit up. " You don't mean at—at Step Down?"

" Oh no! I'm the cook there and Jock's the gardener. But at The Pallant, when it's built, Nan; to help me with the dinner-parties."

" Would you have me?" Anne cried. " I'd like

that even better than staying here! I'd love to cook for you."

" And Jock! You'll cook for him too, I hope." Maidlin smiled at her. " I'd love to have you. You'd be heaps more to me than our cook!"

" I hope she'll go with you," Mary said. " We'd like to feel you had a friend standing by you."

" That's lovely of you, Mary-Dorothy," Anne exclaimed, her face alight.

" You could help to plan the kitchen part of The Pallant," Maidlin added. " We're going to design it ourselves, so you could have just what you want."

" Is it really to be called The Pallant?" Mary asked. " But what does it mean, Maid?"

" We haven't an idea." Maidlin laughed up at her from where she sat on a big tuffet by the fire. " Jock won't call it anything else. Isn't he silly? I tell him he is, but he says he's never had anybody to be silly with before and he likes being silly."

" He looks much younger lately," Mary observed. " You're being very good for him."

" And he for you," she thought, but kept it to herself, as she looked at Maidlin's radiant face, lit up from within. " I wonder what Joy will say to this new Maid? She's unnoticing, but I don't think even Joy could fail to see the change."

Mary waited in quiet eagerness, and the twins and Maidlin in wild excitement, for Joy's arrival. Anne and Lindy, less thrilled, were still keenly interested.

The finding of the berth and the voyage had taken

longer than Joy had expected, however, and the twins were well again when the great day came.

The car drove up late one afternoon. Frost had gone to Liverpool the night before, to be ready to meet the boat early in the morning.

" All well, Frost?" was Joy's anxious greeting.

" Very well, my lady. Miss Margaret is in particularly good form, if I may say so."

Joy laughed. " That sounds as if she's all right again! And Elizabeth?"

" Extremely well." And then, with the privilege of an old friend, who had been one of the family for many years: " You'll find Miss Maidlin changed, my lady. We've all noticed it."

" Oh?" Joy gave him a quick look. " Don't tell me any more! How are you getting on without Mrs. Spindle?"

" Miss Bellanne is a great improvement on Mrs. Spindle," Frost said primly. " Miss Bellanne's puddings and cakes leave nothing to be desired, and her pastry deserves the highest praise."

Joy lay back in the car and laughed. " How jolly of you, Frost! I shall tell Miss Bellanne of your approval. Now get me home as quickly as you can."

" Yes, my lady," and Frost took the car carefully away from the pierhead and then shot off through the country.

The twins, released from quarantine and imprisonment, were dancing with impatience on the terrace, as Joy leaned from the car and waved her hand. With shrieks of joy they rushed to meet her, and Frost had to draw up while still some way down the drive, to let them jump in and hurl themselves on their mother. Then he drove on to the foot of the terrace steps, where Maidlin waited, with Mary, Anne and Lindy in an eager group behind.

" Oh, she is like the twins!" Lindy whispered. " Nan, isn't she lovely?"

" Bobbed red hair, just like theirs," Anne added. " Yes, she's beautiful, and the children are the very image of her. I am glad we're here! Aren't you, Lin?"

" Rather!" Lindy murmured ecstatically. " Such a bit of luck, her coming home just now!"

Mary's eyes went from Maidlin to Joy and she waited expectantly, not knowing that Frost had forestalled her.

Joy had forgotten Frost's warning in the excitement of seizing the twins and looking them over for signs of measles.

" They seem all right!" she called gaily. " But I had to see for myself. You've taken good care of them. Why, Maid! Maidie, my dear!"

" What's the matter, Joy? Oh, it's lovely to have you again!" Maidlin ran into her arms.

" Let me look at you!" Joy commanded. " Maid, what has John Robertson done to you? You're beautiful, child! He's brought you to life. I didn't know you could look like this, Madalena!"

Maidlin, crimson and shining, hid her face on Joy's shoulder. " Joy, I've wanted you so badly. But, Joy, even without you I've been so happy."

" I can believe that." Joy clasped her closely.

" You look as if you'd never been really happy before."

" Joy, how can you? I've always been happy!"

" You've never looked like this. Let me see you again!"

" Look at this!" Maidlin, laughing where once she would have smiled, showed her ruby ring.

" What a beauty! But he's given you more than a ring, Maid."

" Oh yes!" Maidlin said happily. " Something nobody else in the world could have given me. I'm not sure what it is, and it doesn't matter, but I'd have had to go without it if he hadn't come."

" Fulfilment — complete personality," Joy thought. " She was only half herself; now she's come into her kingdom. She's right; none of us could have done it for her. Oh, I am so thankful!"

The twins were trying to make her listen. " Uncle Jock's going to give her a house without any stairs in it," Elizabeth made herself heard.

" We're going to see it to-morrow, and you're coming too!" Margaret shouted. " Won't no upstairs be funny?"

" Aunty Maid says it's a dolly's house. I think Uncle Jock's a very large doll," Elizabeth began.

" Look, Mother! We've got daisy rings, like Aunty Maid's. They're measles-prizes. Mine was for spots; I had most spots. Twin's was for being good and quiet," Margaret sang.

Joy looked at Maidlin with raised eyebrows. " Are your plans made already? Is it to be a bungalow? Is that the best he can do for you? Won't you feel it very cramped after living here?"

"The dolls' house is to be my wedding-present."
Maidlin's old smile glimmered in her happy eyes.
"We're going to build our real house; the baby
house is near the sea, our place of escape when we
want to run away and be alone. Jock's bought it
and he's going to give it to me. Will you come to
see it to-morrow, Joy? The twins are wild to go."

"It's called Step Down, because you fall down
a step at the gate," Margaret explained. "*I* shan't
fall down!"

"The big house is called The Pallant, but they
don't know what it means," Elizabeth added.

Joy looked at Maidlin and went off into a peal
of laughter. "Maidie, how absurd!"

"I know. We're perfectly ridiculous, I about
Step Down and Jock about The Pallant," Maidlin
admitted. "But we're both quite determined and
you can't alter us, so you needn't argue. Won't
you speak to Mary-Dorothy? She's waiting so
patiently for her turn."

Joy's hand shot out to Mary. "My dear, I'm
sorry you've had such a bad time! I've a lot to
say to Susie Spindle. But you've done splendidly;
the twinnies look as well as ever. I'm so thankful
to see them for myself. And you "—she turned to
the other two—" must be the Bellanne girls. I've
heard about you, and I'm more grateful than I can
say for your great help to Mary and Maid in this
crisis."

"I'm the new cook, Lady Quellyn." Anne's
eyes were on her in eager delight. "I'm Nan."

"I'm Lindy, the nursery governess. No, I mean
Miss Belinda." Lindy made a funny little curtsey.

"But aren't you the singer—the skylark Maid found in the Abbey? We mustn't harness you to a schoolroom. I want to hear you sing. If your voice is really good we'll help you to make the most of it, and you'll be the new Jenny Lind, instead of Lindy."

Lindy's eyes blazed. "My name is like hers; I'd never thought of that!"

"I thought of it at once. I'm going to write a song called 'The Lark in the Abbey,' and you shall sing it. Now take me indoors, Twinnies! When am I to see John Robertson, Maid?"

"I wanted him to come to dinner, but he was sure you'd be too tired. He's coming early to-morrow, to take the children to see Step Down; it's been promised to them for some time. If you could come too, Joy, we'd like it so much."

"Of course I'll come. I must see this wonderful bungalow."

"And you will call him Jock!" Maidlin urged. "He likes it so much better. 'John Robertson' sounds outside the family!"

"I'll try to feel he's one of the family," Joy promised. "But he has stolen you away from me, that's certain."

"You won't go away again before May-day, will you, Joy?" Maidlin asked that night, when Joy had come to sit on her bed, and Jock and the future had been discussed.

"I might stay as long as that. It would be fun to see a crowning again."

"Oh, but you'll be taking part! You must be in the procession of Queens this year."

" I think not," Joy laughed. " I'm rather an old married lady to dress up as a May Queen."

" But all the married ones are coming. You don't understand," Maidlin said earnestly. " It's a very special occasion, and however much and often people have been married they're coming to be queens this year. It's the twentieth year of the Hamlet Club, and we're going to crown the twenty-first queen; there were two one year, you know, because the President had to go to Ceylon directly after she'd been crowned."

Joy looked interested. " That is rather an event! Who is the new queen?"

" That's a thrill too. Miriam's girl, little Mirry, is to be queen."

Joy sat up. " The first grandchild of the Club! The first queen's eldest daughter! Oh, I can't resist that! But is little Mirry old enough, Maid?"

" She's twelve. It's young to be queen, but the Club's younger than it used to be—much more a junior thing. The seniors say they're too busy; they're sure they work harder than we did! I don't believe it, but the present fashion at school is to leave the Club to the juniors. Small Mirry is quite a leader and a great favourite."

" Her mother was both. And are the rest of our crowd really going to dress up and be queens again?"

" Miriam must, for Mirry, of course; and Cicely will come with her. Marguerite's still in America, and I'm afraid we can't have Joan, though she may come to watch. But the rest will come. It will make all the difference to have you, Joy."

" Is Rosamund coming?"

" Oh yes! She won't be the Countess for that afternoon; she'll just be Ros, the Rose Queen. You'll forget you're Lady Quellyn and be ' Traveller's Joy,' and Jen will forget she's Lady Marchwood and be our Jenny-Wren, or Queen Brownie."

" It sounds great fun," Joy admitted. " I wonder where my green robe has been put?"

" It's ready," Maidlin said eagerly. " Mary found it and it's been cleaned and pressed. I've hoped so much that you'd join in, Joy."

" Would I be allowed to have the twinnies as my maids-of-honour?" Joy asked, laughing.

" You must, of course. I was going to have one of them and Ros the other, but we'll ask somebody else."

" But—Maid! Oughtn't we to have people from the school?"

" Not this year. Everybody's going to have a daughter, if she has a daughter old enough to walk. That's one of the new ideas for the very special occasion. Miriam will have her second girl, little Cicely, who's eight; and the President will have her own Cicely, who is almost nine. Jen's trying to persuade Rosemary to come with her, but you know how shy Rosemary is, and after all she isn't five yet. Jen says perhaps she'll bring Andrew and have a page instead of a maid-of-honour. But nobody can have two maids-of-honour but you! Joy, you must come, for th sake of the twins. People will love to see you with two train-bearers!"

" I really think I shall have to do it," Joy exclaimed. " But what about you and Rosamund?"

" We'll find somebody. Ros agreed that her red colours would look terrible on a twin, though Margaret was charmed to hear she'd have to wear a red girdle."

" Oh, you couldn't have allowed that! She'd have had to have white. Your yellow would have been lovely for Elizabeth."

" They'll both wear your green. It will add enormously to May Day to have you there!"

" Are husbands and fathers invited? Can John Robertson come to see you being a queen?"

" Jock, Joy!"

" Sorry—Jock! He ought to see you dance."

" He'll come. I've invited him," Maidlin said happily. " Joy, won't you go and talk to Mary before you go to bed?"

Joy, on her way to the door, looked back at her with raised brows. " I believe I'd like to do that. But I never have gone to Mary's room at night as much as the rest of you."

" Mary would love it. You must want somebody besides me to talk to. Jen will be home tomorrow, but for to-night, Joy——!"

Joy laughed and came back to stand staring down at her. " Now, Maid! How did you know? Of course I want to talk things over with somebody, and as I can't have Jen I'd love to go to Mary. But I thought perhaps it wasn't fair to you. We shall talk about you; we couldn't possibly help it. Don't you mind?"

" I *want* you to talk about me!" Maidlin snuggled down under the bedclothes with a sup-

pressed chuckle. " I know you're dying to do it.
But it would be much more fun for you to talk
about Jock! Mary simply loves him; she'll tell
you so. I want you to hear how nice he is from
somebody else. I know you think I'm daft about
him."

" Oh—Maid!" Joy laughed in protest, and bent
and kissed her.

" It's so wonderful!" Maidlin whispered. " To
feel I matter more than any one else to him. I've
never come first with anybody before. It's a marvellous feeling, Joy!"

" Oh, my dear, I know! And I am so glad."
Joy kissed her again, and went off to Mary's room.

Mary's face lit up at sight of her. " Joy, how
lovely of you to come!"

Joy took Jen's old seat beside the gas-ring.
" Coffee—yes, thank you, Mary-Dorothy! What
a time you've been through, without any one to
back you up! Didn't the sudden appearance of
this new Maidlin stun you completely?"

Mary, busy with brown and gold cups and
saucers, smiled across at her. " I was terrified.
Maid's so sensitive, and she goes to such extremes.
I was afraid of doing or saying the wrong thing and
spoiling everything."

Joy took her cup with a word of thanks. " Extremes! You're right there. She isn't like herself
at all."

" Oh, I think she is! She always goes to the
absolute limit when her feelings are stirred. Think
of her passionate love for you—and her despair
when Andrew took her place—and her distress over

the trouble with Rosamund—and her flight from you when Ivor appeared!''

Joy coloured. '' That was my fault. But I see what you mean. Maid has always overdone things; I suppose she isn't quite balanced in her feelings.''

'' Of course not. She's never felt she had a safe anchorage till now. People have failed her by falling in love with someone else; or have misunderstood her. For the first time in her life she's feeling secure.''

Joy looked at her. '' It's rather wonderful, Mary. She's just said to me that it was marvellous to feel she came first with somebody.''

Mary sat down, cup in hand. '' Yes, I've heard her say that. I'm so very thankful it has come to her. Do you wonder at the change in her? She's so radiantly happy; she can't keep it in. Presently she'll settle down and be her quiet self again, but with a new depth of happiness. But just now she's lifted above herself, and it must show.''

'' I see,'' Joy said thoughtfully. '' I've been rejoicing in her happiness, but I had a shade of regret because my dear dreamy Maid had vanished.''

'' She's awake now. It's a thing to be thankful for. I've wondered at times how things would go with her. She was content with her home and her music, and you and the children, and her beloved Abbey. But she wouldn't have been satisfied for ever. She was bound to awake some day to the fact that all the rest of you had homes of your own, and husbands and children, and that, however happy she might be, she was sharing your home

and your children. And the twins would have
grown up and no longer have needed her. Maid
would have been left with her singing and the
Abbey, and with a lonely little feeling of regret,
of something she had missed. It wasn't enough;
she had this wealth of love and trust to give to
somebody. I'm more thankful than I can say that
she has found the right man, who understands her
as no one has ever done yet."

" She said," Joy laughed, " that you would
tell me how nice he is, because I'd consider her daft
about him. She says you simply love him. Tell
me more about him, Mary! I know him, of course,
but I rather think he must be a new person too.
Has Maid worked a miracle in him, as well as he
in her?"

" The miracle of the butterfly from the chrysalis;
perhaps she has. But I didn't know him before."

" It's that with Maid, anyway. He always
seemed to me rather quiet and shy. Tell me about
them both, when they're together, Mary!"

" *How* Maid will enjoy having a home of her
own!" Mary smiled. " All her life she has lived
in other people's houses. You can see what she
feels in her radiant delight over this dolls' house
bungalow." And she told what she could of Jock's
coming and of Maidlin's happiness, while Joy
listened in rapt interest and sympathy.

CHAPTER XXIII

PASSING ON THE TORCH

WILD with excitement, the twins sprang from the car, ran to the gate of the little house, and promptly fell down the long step into the garden path. Margaret, with a whoop of delight, leapt out to the street to do it again, and fell down three times before she would allow the others to enter. Elizabeth stood by the gate and warned her mother to be careful.

" We feel it will be so kind of us to put ' Step Down ' on the gate," Maidlin explained, as they went to the glass door.

Saying he had an errand to do in the town, which lay between the house and the sea, Jock went off in the car for half an hour, after he and Maidlin together had done the honours of the little place. The children rushed up and down the passage and in and out of the rooms and of the garden door, and Joy and Maidlin hoisted themselves on to the broad window-sill of the bedroom and sat in the sunshine.

" All the windows have these wide ledges. I do think they're nice," Maidlin said.

" Maid, it's quite charming—as a week-end cottage, of course," Joy assured her. " You must have a bigger place for your home, but for holidays you couldn't have anything nicer than this."

" I'm so glad you've seen it, Joy. Now you'll

know what I'm talking about in my letters. Must you really go back soon?"

"Quite soon. There's a big garden-party to which we must go, and other engagements that Ivor wants me for; and I mustn't neglect David for too long. But we'll be home again in July, and I'm thinking seriously of taking the twinnies back with me for the winter. They ought to see New York, and New York ought to see them! Our friends there refuse to believe that I have daughters of nine years old."

"They won't refuse to believe it once they've seen the twinnies," Maidlin remarked. "They couldn't be anybody's daughters but yours."

"Or Joan's; but New York doesn't know Joan. I really think the children should go with us in the autumn. Then next year we can think about school in earnest. I meant you to come too, but I suppose Jock would have something to say to that."

"He wants——" Maidlin began, and stopped.

"He wants you in the autumn. You'll have to decide. Why has he run away into the town?"

"He said he'd tell us when he came back. I shouldn't wonder if it was to fetch ices for the children," Maidlin smiled. "There he is! He hasn't been long."

Laden with ices for all, Jock came in triumphantly.

"I've found it! Here, Marchwood Twins, put these away—you know where."

"Inside us!" The twins seized their tubs with whoops of joy.

" What have you found to make you look so cock-a-hoop?" Joy asked, sitting perched on the ledge to eat her ice.

" The meaning of Pallant. I've been hunting it for days."

" Oh, tell us!" Maidlin cried. " Is it a pigsty?"

" Let me break it to you gently. The Pallant is The Palace."

" Oh, Jock!" Maidlin rocked with laughter. " We can't call our house The Palace!"

" If you're not careful you'll fall off that sill," he warned her. " My ' Doctor ' doesn't mean I'm qualified to set broken limbs, you know."

" Does it really mean Palace, Jock? How did you find out? Is that what you went into the town for?"

" The library here has a good Sussex room. Pallant is a Sussex word—at least, it seems to be used only in Sussex—so I stalked in and demanded the meaning. They were most kind and helpful and brought dictionaries. Pallant is the Old English form of palace—palente. A palace is a dwelling or an enclosure; didn't you know? It's a most suitable name for a house."

" It would be lovely, of course," Maidlin agreed. " Our enclosed place, that we've made for ourselves. Oh, I like that!"

" A palace is a place enclosed by a palisade, or a paling. We'll put a paling round our Pallant, and you'll be the little sheep kept inside the palace. There's a fascinating derivation from Pal-es, the Roman god of flocks and shepherds; palace was first used for a dwelling on the Palatine Hill of

Rome, and the hill was called after the god Pal-es.
There's no help for it, Maid; you'll have to welcome all our guests at The Pallant with songs about
feeding flocks.''

Maidlin's laugh rang out again. " People would
get sick of me! But I like your ancient history;
you have worked hard! And I'll be your sheep in
your palace!''

" Maid, you laugh much oftener than you did,"
Joy remarked. " You used just to smile at us.''

Maidlin's eyes met Jock's, and they both smiled.
" So does he. I've told him so," she said.

Joy nodded and turned to Jock. " Why is your
funny word used only in Sussex?''

" I suppose Sussex is rather Old English; it is,
you know, in its place-names. But the real reason
is that in Chichester the Archbishop had special
rights over a part of the city, close to the cathedral
—palatine rights is the correct expression—and this
part is called The Pallant. I said from the first it
was ecclesiastical and dignified; Maid, having a
low mind, was sure it would turn out to mean a
pigsty. The Pallant, or The Palace, is the enclosure
to which the palatine rights belong. But the word
is used as a name for a house, so our house, when
it's built, will be The Pallant.''

" I like it," Maidlin said contentedly. " How
clever of you to find such a jolly meaning! I'll
like to live at The Pallant. Joy, we shall choose a
place for it between you and Rosamund, so that
I can have you both quickly when I want you.
And Jock's promised that at least once in each week
he'll take me to the Abbey for the whole day, while

he goes to town to take his singing pupils and see
to rehearsals for concerts. I shan't really be far
away. Now we ought to go home." She turned to
Jock. " We're expecting streams of visitors to see
Joy, and this morning Rosamund rang up to ask
if she might come at tea-time. We couldn't give
up our trip to Step Down, but we ought to hurry
back."

" Having a picnic lunch at your beloved Rose
and Squirrel on the way. That's agreed on," he
said. " Say good-bye to your dolls' house, then.
Hear those children careering about!"

" They've never been in an empty house before.
It has gone to Margaret's head." Joy laughed, and
called the twins out to the car.

" Joy, did you notice the name of the road?"
Maidlin asked, as the car turned into the London
by-pass.

" No? I never look at names of streets when
I'm in a car."

" I didn't see it at first. It's St. Michael's
Avenue!" She looked at Joy expectantly.

" It sounds like our Abbey."

" That's the point." Maidlin gave her old
glimmer of a smile. " All the roads round here are
saints: St. Lawrence, and St. Thomas, and St.
George's Road; it's lovely that our house should
be in St. Michael's Avenue."

" The first Abbot of the Abbey was Michael,"
Joy agreed. " You'll appreciate that, I know."

" I said Jock must have done it on purpose, so
that I'd feel linked up with the Abbey, even at Step

Down," Maidlin laughed. " But he admits it's just an accident."

Rosamund was still talking with Joy after tea when another visitor arrived. She rose to go, but Maidlin laid a hand on her arm. " Come into the Abbey with me," she pleaded.

" I'd like to. I always want a look at the dear old place," Rosamund agreed. " How do you feel about leaving it, Maid? Very bad? I felt dreadful, and you care even more than I did."

" That's what I want to talk about." Maidlin's face was sober as they went through the Abbot's garden, where the blue pansies were in flower.

They held memories for Rosamund and she smiled at them as she passed. Through the tresaunt to the garth she followed Maidlin. " Now, Maid, tell me! This is the right place."

" Margaret would want us to go into the dark little parlour. She insists it is the talking-place," Maidlin said. " But I'd rather have the garth and the sunshine. Ros, I shall feel bad at leaving all this, and the dear Hall, just as you did, but I shall come back often. That's not the trouble. I'm ready to leave anything for Jock, or of course I wouldn't be willing to marry him at all."

" Of course not," Rosamund laughed at her. " Well, Maid?"

" It's what we said when we came in here a year ago, when you were on your way to Kentisbury for the first time. You told me to bear the torch, as everyone else had had to go away, and we said that the torch meant welcoming people who came here in trouble."

" Well, you've done it. Look how good you've been to your little singing girl and her sister ! "

" Think how helpful they've been to us ! I don't know what we should have done without them. Lindy says it was Bellannes to the rescue, and it really was. But I can't do it any more, Ros. What about the torch?   Is it quite right for me to be married and go away? Sometimes I wonder if I'm a deserter, and if I ought to stay here."

Rosamund's laugh rang out, but the laugh was not a hurtful one. " Maid dearest, how like you ! You would wonder if it was right. But you mean to do it, right or wrong, I hope?"

" No," Maidlin pondered her answer and spoke slowly. " I mean to do it because I feel it's right— for me to marry Jock, I mean. But I'm puzzled about the torch."

" But the torchbearers of old never went on carrying the torch for ever," Rosamund said gently. " When each had done his turn he handed it to a fresh runner. You've done your share; now you pass on the torch to someone else."

" I see." There was great content in Maidlin's voice. " It's right to lay it down?"

" Absolutely right. Someone else will pick it up and take on the job for you."

" I wonder who? Oughtn't I to find the right person and explain to her?"

" No, don't do that," Rosamund said. " You, and I, and all of us weren't self-conscious about it; we didn't realise what we were doing for a long while. That's the best way, Maid. Leave it to the Abbey to find its own interpreter ! "

Maidlin's eyes lit up. " You mean, let the Abbey take hold of somebody so that she has to carry on its tradition without understanding what she's doing?"

" Isn't that how it happened with us?"

" Yes, of course it is! If I go to somebody and ask her—no, it wouldn't be the same thing. I see!"

" You've done the job well. Now you must stand back and watch. I don't believe the Abbey tradition of helpfulness and welcome will die out."

" It couldn't, of course. You are a comfort, Ros! I do like that idea. I wonder who it will be?"

" Your little Lindy may grow into the deeper meaning of the Abbey, if she stays here; or her pretty sister."

" Oh, but Anne's going to take care of Jock and me at The Pallant! And Lindy's going to sing."

" They'll both be here for a little while, and then someone else may appear. Red-haired Cecily may come home; she loves every stone of the Abbey. And there's always Mary-Dorothy, waiting quietly in the background till she's needed."

" I hadn't forgotten Mary, but she has so many other things to do. I'm glad I asked you, Ros. I feel much better about getting married now."

Rosamund laughed again, but her eyes were very kindly as she said: " I'm glad to have been able to relieve your mind! Have you discussed it with your Jock?"

" I want to, but I've been waiting till I'd talked to you. I wanted to be clear in my own mind before I told him. He knows how much I love the Abbey and how sorry I'll be to leave it, and he'll bring me back often. But I haven't told him about the torch yet. I haven't talked about it to anybody. It's between you and me, Ros."

" How like you, Maid! Not Joy?"

" Joy would laugh. She wouldn't understand."

" I think perhaps she would now," Rosamund said. " But you don't talk about the things you feel most deeply, do you?"

" Only to Jock. That's why he's so useful."

" Good for Jock! He's made himself useful to you very quickly. But, Maid, dear, there's another side to all that we've been saying. You're going to kindle the torch in a new place. All your plans for your home show that. You and Jock are going to help struggling musicians and welcome lonely beginners; what's that but bearing the Abbey torch in a fresh place?"

Maidlin's face lit up. " I'd thought of that. I shall try to take that bit of the Abbey wherever I go."

" And that shows it's right for you to go away. You can do more, now, by starting in a new home. I hope to find chances to do it at Kentisbury too. The Abbey inspires and trains us, Maid, and then we go to our new homes to carry on."

Maidlin's face was very bright as they went back to the Hall. " Jock will understand all that when I tell him. He's very keen on finding and helping beginners and people who have failed or who haven't had a good chance."

" You and Jock will do the job well," Rosamund agreed. " Your house will be a real new centre for the Abbey torch."

" Ros, Joy's coming to school on May Day. Won't it be lovely to have her?"

" Oh, good! I hoped she would. Geoffrey's coming to look on; he's frightfully amused at the thought of seeing me as a May Queen!"

" Jock thinks it's funny too. I don't know why! But he says he wants to see me wearing a crown."

" They think we ought to have put schoolgirl things behind us. But they don't know what the Hamlet Club has meant to all of us; everything, even our friendships. I must find a new maid."

" Yes, the twinnies are booked. They're fearfully thrilled. Whom shall you have?" Maidlin asked.

" Young Tansy, from the Castle. She'll be thrilled, if you like!"

" Oh, that's nice! I shall ask Lindy Bellanne. She's to be our first musical child, to be trained and launched on her career."

" Good! She'll be proud. I saw her with the twins; she seems to manage them very well."

" Beautifully. Joy's so pleased about her and Nan."

" And you're going to carry them both off to your palace!" Rosamund had heard the plans for the new house.

" They belong to me. Joy can find somebody else," Maidlin said simply.

CHAPTER XXIV

MAIDING MAID

" COME into my room, Miss Belinda!" Maidlin
invited the nursery governess when the children
were in bed. " Now, Lindy Bellanne, will you be
my maid-of-honour and carry my train at the school
coronation on May Day?"

" I?" Lindy's face blazed in delight. " Oh,
Miss Maid! Would you have me?"

" The people who can manage it will have
daughters. The next best thing is to have a girl
one is interested in. I'm interested in you, Miss
Belinda," Maidlin said laughing. " You're going
to belong to us, so far as your training is concerned.
What could be more suitable?"

" How I'll love it! I remember thinking it was
a rapturous prospect, when I heard we were coming
here to stay, but this is much more rapturous than
I'd ever dreamed of!"

" I've seen your white frock; it will do quite
well. You'll need a girdle of my colours. I'm the
Primrose Queen; you'll hear me called Primrose
at school. We'll find some yellow and pale-green
ribbons and make a belt for you. You won't have
much to do, and there will be other strangers among
the train-bearers. You'll watch the rest and copy
them."

Lindy, radiant, raced off to tell the news to Anne,
and for the next week she went about in a happy

dream, and discussed May Day revels with the twins at every opportunity.

When the great day came, the Hall forgot that it was a staid grown-up house and became a centre of schoolgirl excitement. The morning was given up to making wreaths of spring flowers for the maids-of-honour and crowns for Joy and Maidlin, and to packing white robes and gaily-coloured trains, and arranging great shower bouquets for the queens to carry.

In the midst of the feverish activity there came a wail of distress from Margaret. " My daisy ring's gone! It's fallen off me! Oh, Twin, come an' look for it, quick!"

" It's here." Elizabeth picked up the treasure from the floor. " Looks as if you'd been jumping on it, silly girl. It's squashed all to bits."

" 'Tisn't—it mustn't be! Oh, it *is*!" Margaret broke into heart-broken sobbing. " It's spoilt—Mother, look!"

" Don't cry like that, darling. We'll get you another," Joy said.

" Oh, you can't do that sort of thing!" Lindy burst out in horror.

Joy looked at her, raising her brows in amusement. " The stern governess! Do you think I spoil the twins?"

Lindy grew crimson. " I oughtn't to have said it. But Margaret's so careless; she'll never learn to be careful if you just buy her another."

" What do you think I ought to do, then?"

" Let her save up and buy another ring. You

could help her a little; but she ought to do most of it herself," Lindy said promptly.

Joy looked at her daughters. "Twinnies, you hear that? I have spoiled you; everybody says so. Shall we take Miss Belinda's advice and behave properly? Will you save up and buy another ring, Margaret?"

"I'll help you, Twin," Elizabeth said generously. "If Miss Belinda wants us to, I s'pose we'll have to do it."

"But you'll have a ring on when you carry Mother's train, and I won't," Margaret wept. "I was going to stick out my finger so that everybody would see I'd got a ring."

"Then you can just stick your finger in again into its proper place and not try to show off!" Elizabeth said tartly.

"Twin, if you didn't have on any ring," Margaret hinted, "it wouldn't matter a bit then! Oh, Twin! Be a sport!"

Joy and Maidlin and Lindy, thrilled but silent, watched Elizabeth's struggle with herself. With a sigh she drew off her daisy ring. "All right, Twin. We won't either of us have rings. That's the best plan. I'll put mine away in a box till you've bought another one."

"Oh, goody! Thank you, Elizabeth-Twin!" and Margaret danced about the hall in her relief.

"Come and put my ring away," Elizabeth said sadly, and the twins went up the staircase, their arms round one another.

"Good for Elizabeth!" Lindy murmured. "She's a sport, right enough!"

" Rather nice of her." Joy's voice was full of pride.

" Much better than if you'd bought Margaret another ring. Miss Belinda gave Elizabeth her chance and she rose to the occasion," Maidlin agreed. " Oh, there's the phone!" She went to answer the call. " It's for you, Joy. It's Joan speaking."

Joy talked eagerly for some minutes, then came to report delightedly to Maidlin.

" Joan's coming, after all. I tried hard to per-suade her when I saw her last week. She'll bring Jansy as her maid, so the family will be complete."

" Coming as queen?" Maidlin cried.

" Of course. She's quite well and she says there's no reason why she shouldn't. It will make the day perfect to have her."

" Who is she? Why does she matter so much?" Lindy looked up from her flowers.

The twins, who had returned while Joy was at the phone, looked shocked. " The Abbey's hers, Aunty Lin. Didn't you know?"

" You never told me that. I thought it was yours. Why is it hers, when it's in your garden?" Lindy looked at Joy.

" The Abbey part belongs to Joan," Maidlin said. " We ought to have explained that to you long ago."

" It shows what a very new friend you are, Lindy Bellanne," Joy said. " Joan is my cousin, and we were brought up together, and when we were at school people used to take us for twins. Her Jansy is exactly like Elizabeth and Margaret, so there will be five of us.''

'' Five all just the same to look at,'' Margaret sang. '' It will be nice to see Jansy.''

'' Will people laugh?'' Elizabeth asked, amused.

'' I shouldn't wonder. If they do, you mustn't laugh back. You must remember you're being maids-of-honour and everybody's looking at you.''

'' We will, Mother, we will!'' the twins cried together.

'' I'll see that they do,'' Lindy promised. '' Don't forget that Miss Belinda's going to be there, keeping a stern eye on you, my little dears.''

The twins shouted with glee. '' We like you when you're being Miss Belinda!''

Presently Maidlin was whirled away to school by Dr. Jock in his car, laden with flowers, crown, and royal robes; and Lindy was invited to sit in the back seat with the luggage. Joy and the twins, and Anne and Mary, followed in the big car, driven by Frost, and joined Lindy and Maidlin in the excited clamour of the dressing-room.

Lindy, intensely interested, drew the twins into a corner, to leave Joy free to greet her friends, and questioned the children about each new arrival. Elizabeth and Margaret had been to May Day festivals before, as onlookers, and they knew all the former queens and many of the maids-of-honour.

'' That's the White Queen—the new Queen Mirry is her little girl. That's the President; she started the Club and the country-dancing and made them have queens each year. Here comes our Aunty

Jen!'' as a very tall curly-headed queen in a bright brown train and a crown of cowslips came in. '' Oh! Oh! There's Jansy and Aunty Joan!''

'' Gosh!'' gasped Lindy. '' It might just as well be Lady Quellyn and one of you!'' For Joan Raymond, wearing a loose white robe and a rich violet train, and carrying a great shower bouquet of branches of early lilac, was like another Joy, and her red-haired maid-of-honour might well have been a twin.

'' Jansy's hair's longer than ours and Aunty Joan isn't bobbed, like Mother is,'' Elizabeth explained.

Rosamund came in, wearing a crimson train and carrying red roses from her greenhouses, followed by a black-haired schoolgirl of fourteen, at sight of whom the twins gave a united stifled shriek of joy. '' It's Tansy, from the Castle!''

Tansy's eyes found them, and she grinned a joyful greeting. But the procession was forming, and there was no time to speak.

The mother of the new little queen, who had been the first to reign over the Hamlet Club, and was now receiving congratulations on her daughter's promotion, led the long line; then came the President, in her golden train, and Joy, wearing bright green. Joan, in her violet robe, smiled an amused acknowledgment of the delighted shouts of the crowd, who had feared she would not come. Blue queen and silver queen, '' Queen Beetle '' in gaudy stripes, Queen Barbara in cream, with wild roses on her train, brought Rosamund, with Tansy holding up her crimson robe. Jen, Lady Marchwood, was attended by a small fair-haired son, the twins' cousin Andrew, who held himself sturdily, though he was the only page in the procession; and then Lindy found herself walking up the hall, carrying Maidlin's primrose train, with its border of green.

Each queen was received with cheers, but when Joy appeared with two small attendants, the shouts swelled into a roar of delight; and the twins, each holding a corner of the apple-green train, beamed in return and looked around without a trace of shyness. As the long row of queens took their places on the dais, with their maids seated at their feet, both Lindy and Tansy, on one side, looked not at the new little queen coming to be crowned, wearing a train of forget-me-not blue, but at the other side of the platform, where two queens and three maids sat together, and every one of the five was as much like the others as peas in a pod.

" Five of them! " Lindy murmured joyfully.

Tansy edged closer to her. " They've never all been here together before, My Lady says. Don't they look funny, all alike? But lovely, of course."

" The twins have told me about you," Lindy said cautiously, under cover of the cheering for little Mirry.

" I've heard about you from My Lady. You sing, don't you?"

" I'm going to learn from Miss Maid. But just now I'm Miss Belinda, the nursery governess. Lady Joy laughs at my name; she once had a motor-bike called Belinda, and she had an accident and nearly killed Lady Jen."

"I hadn't heard about that. Do the twins like having a governess?"

"It was their own plan," Lindy grinned at her. "They might not have liked me if I'd been shoved at them. Miss Maid and Lady Joy say they'd put off finding a governess for fear the kiddies wouldn't like the idea, and if they didn't they'd be dreadful, of course. But they thought of it for themselves, and asked me to be Miss Belinda, so they're frightfully pleased about me, really. What are you going to do?"

"Be My Lady's housekeeper and take care of the Castle and everybody. I'll have a marvellous time."

"Oh! Rather jolly, I should think!"

"Yes, super-wonderful. I'm terribly keen. How lovely Queen Maidlin looks to-day! Which is the man she's going to marry?"

Lindy described Dr. Jock's position in the audience, and Tansy gazed at him critically.

"He looks very jolly. Is he good enough for her?"

"She seems to think so. I heard her say to Lady Joy, ' Of course, I'm not *nearly* good enough for him!' "

"Oh, bosh! He's watching her all the time; he never looks at anybody else. He'll like to see her dance."

"How can they dance country-dances in those long frocks?"

"My Lady says they'll change. Mrs. Raymond won't dance, of course; I expect she'll watch and then go home. It was nice of her to come. My Lady didn't know she'd be here; she was frightfully pleased to see her."

" Lady Joy and Miss Maid only heard this morning. They were glad too."

" The twins are being very good. I thought they'd get playing about with Jansy Raymond."

" They know I'm looking at them. What's the other one's real name?"

" Janice. She's their cousin. There's a boy, John, and a baby girl, Jennifer, as well. They live not far from the Castle, and they sometimes come to tea with us."

" What's happening now? Have you seen all this before?"

" No, but My Lady told me what they'd do. It's the maypole. After they've danced and plaited the ribbons and shown a few special things, like morris dances, the queens will change and everybody will join in for country-dancing. You and I will have to help our queens out of their robes, and then fold them up and pack them carefully."

" I shall help Lady Joy too. The twins won't be much use as maids."

However, Mary was there to help Joy, and the changing was over very quickly. The queens who wanted to dance had brought short frocks, and they seemed like schoolgirls again as they ran out to join in the sets. Maidlin looked startlingly different in vivid rose pink, Joy kept to her favourite green, Rosamund and Jen wore blue. The maids-of-honour were already dancing, and Lindy, following the queens, saw Elizabeth and Jansy skipping up the middle of a set together and then swinging wildly, next to Andrew and Margaret.

" Have ' Newcastle ' with me, Ros!" Maidlin cried gaily.

" One with you and one with Joy," Rosamund said. " Perhaps a little one with Jenny-Wren, for old times' sake. Then I must rush back to my young viscount. He'll raise the roof if I keep him waiting."

" Of Kentisbury Castle? Oh, *Ros*!"

" Good sound lungs Lord Verriton must have," the President remarked.

" His lungs are all right. He yells the place down if he doesn't get what he wants. But we're training him, aren't we, Tansy?"

" He's a marvellous baby," Tansy said.

" It's fun, isn't it, Jock? Won't you learn to dance?" Maidlin laughed, running to him, after she had danced " The Geud Man " with Joy.

" I know now where you learned that fascinating curtsey you made to Her Majesty," he said.

" Oh, but we only bob in country-dancing! You must have seen that!" For the last two dances round the maypole had been " Chelsea Reach " and " Oranges and Lemons."

" You made an amazing curtsey to the new queen a few minutes ago. But it's the whole of it, the wonderful musical movement. You're a beautiful thing when you dance, like a roseleaf in the wind. Go and do some more! I want to watch you."

" Much better learn to dance with me!" Maidlin retorted, and turned to claim Jen as a partner.

Since her engagement had been announced, she
had been receiving letters and phone calls continually, but owing to the quarantine at the Hall, this
was the first time her old friends had seen her, and
congratulations and good wishes were hurled at
her on every side, as she met one after another in
the course of longways dances. Joy, with mischief
in her eyes, asked for " Haste to the Wedding,"
and had led Maidlin to the top of a set before Maid
had realised what was happening.

" What are we doing next? Oh, Joy! How
could you?" Maidlin cried, as she heard the tune.

" *For* you; and *with* me. Of course we must,"
Joy said firmly.

There was a cheer as partners were seized and
dragged to the lines. " ' Haste,' for Maid! Come
on! Come and dance for Primrose's wedding!"

Lindy made her way to Dr. Jock's side. " It's
' Haste to the Wedding ' for Miss Maid and you.
I heard them say so."

He looked down at her and laughed. " She's
being ragged by everybody she meets. It's too bad.
Isn't it a joy to see her dance? She's a marvel."

" She looks lovely to-day," Lindy said shyly.

" Oh yes!" he assented, his eyes on Maidlin's
slight figure. " She's as light as dandelion seed.
I must tell her so."

" Wasn't it odd to have strangers in the procession?" The first Queen dropped out of the dance
when she reached the end of the set. " Oh, I'm
hot! But I had to dance for Maidie. You're a
stranger," and she looked at Lindy. " I saw you
maiding Maid, and you're wearing her colours."

" Maiding Maid! I like that. She's adopted me," Lindy said happily.

Queen Miriam the First raised her eyebrows. " Aren't you rather a large adopted child for Maidlin?"

" In music, you know. She's going to teach me to sing."

" Oh, I see!" Miriam, a singer herself, was interested at once. " If Maid has discovered a new voice as well as a husband she'll be very thrilled. She's been having a busy time, finding adventures of all sorts!"

" She's happy, anyway," Lindy ventured.

" Maid, you have plunged into a big new adventure! Somehow I didn't think you'd ever marry," Miriam said, as Maidlin and Joy reached the end of the set and the M.C. called " last time."

Maidlin's eyes danced. " Neither did I. I thought I had everything anybody could want. But I didn't know the world held—Jock!"

" Good for you, Primrose!" Miriam cried, laughing.

" You weren't meant to hear that," Joy informed Dr. Jock, as he threw back his head and gave a shout of laughter.

" Oh, yes, I meant him to hear. He knows!" Maidlin retorted. " He didn't expect to marry either. He's just as much surprised as I am. Oh, Joan's going; she's calling Jansy. Couldn't we give her a send-off, just to cheer her up?"

" She doesn't look as if she needed it." But Joy led the Club in a round of applause for Joan, who had been a much-loved queen.

Joan, draped in her violet robe and holding her branches of lilac carefully before her, bowed a laughing farewell from the platform and withdrew to change and drive home. The dancing began again, and Dr. Jock and Lindy found places on the platform and watched one small pink dancer through the figures of " The Old Mole " and " Hey, Boys " and " Merry Milkmaids."

Tired but happy, they ended at last with a huge ring for " Sellenger's Round."

" If you'd been a dancer they'd have tried to get us into the middle for that last one," Maidlin said, as Jock helped her to stow her flowers and suitcase in the car. " They love to have a victim, and an engaged couple's best of all."

" I'd have died of shyness," he said. " It's a good thing I'm not a dancer."

" Lady Joy wants me to squeeze into the other car and let you two go home alone," Lindy said. " Oh, Miss Maid, thank you for letting me maid you! I've loved doing it."

" Do it again next year, Lindy Bellanne." Maidlin's eyes laughed at her from inside the car. " Married or not, I shall try to come to be the Primrose Queen. I'd like to have you to maid me!"

Late at night Lindy crept into Anne's bedroom. " Nan, did I say, a month ago, that just to think of staying here for a fortnight was a rapturous prospect?"

" You did. Has it come up to your expectations?"

" You know it's been far better than I ever dreamt of. It's the loveliest place and the most

marvellous people in it. And we aren't going away;
not really. I'm one of Miss Maid's new adventures,
and Dr. Jock's the other. They told me a secret in
the car, on the way to the crowning; it was only
decided last night. They're going to be married
in the autumn, when Lady Joy comes back next
time, and then, after they've been to Scotland, she's
going to lend them this house to live in while they
build their own. She'll be in New York, and perhaps the twins will go with her, and there'll be
nobody here except Mary-Dorothy and us; Miss
Maid wants us to stay. So Dr. Jock and she will
live here until The Pallant is ready, and have week-
ends at Step Down, and Miss Maid says she'll be
able to take care of the Abbey for a little while
longer; she seemed quite thrilled about it. I asked
what she meant, for there's the caretaker in the
Abbey; but she just gave me that funny deep smile
and didn't say any more, except that perhaps I'd
find out later on. Isn't it all beautifully arranged?
It's going to be more rapturous than I'd ever
thought anything could be. And I'll make good,
to please Miss Maid, or my name's not Belinda
Bellanne!''

THE END